SECRETS REVEALED

WAR GIRLS, BOOK 8

MARION KUMMEROW

CONTENTS

READER GROUP

Marion's Reader Group

Sign up for my reader group to receive exclusive background information and be the first one to know when a new book is released.

http://kummerow.info/subscribe

CHAPTER 1

Stavanger, Norway, April 1945

L otte sat in the small radio room, discreetly located in one of the old buildings that lined the rocky cliffs of the seashore. After her first, rather turbulent, deployment to Warsaw, both she and her friend, Gerlinde, had been sent to Stavanger six months before. During the long and dark winter months up here in the north of Europe, she'd become acquainted with the rough climate and the rugged landscape.

But the breathtaking scenic beauty of this region with its mountains and fjords couldn't fool her. Stavanger had stopped being a peaceful harbor town in 1940. Several grueling weeks of resistance by the Norwegians hadn't been enough to counter the German invasion.

Since then the ice-free harbors along the Norwegian

coastline had been transformed into strategic military bases. Bases from where destroyers, U-boats and Stuka fighters were launched into the North Sea to find and sink the British convoys on the Arctic route, attempting to sever the supply of much-needed material to the Russians who were fighting the German Wehrmacht with all they had in the East.

During her time there, Morse code had become a second language to her. She didn't have to think about it as her fingers skillfully tapped out the perfectly timed dots and dashes, relaying war-critical information. Sitting at her familiar place in the radio room, she spent her days transmitting encrypted messages to Headquarters.

"Break time," her superior Oberführerin Littmann called out and she finished tapping the message in front of her, before she stood, smoothing down her uniform skirt.

Gerlinde already waited at the door, in the field gray uniform of a Wehrmachtshelferin, a female auxiliary to the Wehrmacht. Lotte always thought the uniform looked much better on Gerlinde, who filled it to perfection with her voluptuous hourglass figure. The skirt ended a hand's width beneath the knee – too short for Oberführerin Littmann's conservative tastes. Gerlinde always explained this with her longer than average legs, but Lotte knew the secrets of her best friend and roommate. Late at night, she would shorten the hem of her skirt just an almost imperceptible inch.

Because, as Gerlinde liked to say, she wouldn't be caught dead in a skirt reaching beyond mid-calf. And she most certainly wouldn't live in a garrison full of young and handsome soldiers wearing such an unfashionable garment.

Lotte herself couldn't care less about admiring male gazes, because she was deeply and completely in love with Johann.

The golden *Reichsadler* on the chest of Gerlinde's – clandestinely tailored – uniform jacket radiated almost like the sunshine itself. And the cap called a *Schiffchen* always accurately adorned her head with that slight tip to one side that made it look chic instead of drab.

Lotte almost laughed out loud. Even during the heated battle in the Warsaw Uprising, Gerlinde had looked like the immaculate models on one of the fashion magazines imported from Paris. But apart from her superficiality, Gerlinde was the best friend she could wish for.

"Alex, what are you waiting for? Or do you want to dawdle our break away in this bleak hole?" Gerlinde called out, jerking Lotte from her thoughts.

Even after living under her new identity of Alexandra Wagner for more than a year, it still felt odd to be called by that name.

"I'm coming." She grabbed her coat and followed Gerlinde into the chilly sea breeze. With longing she looked out at the ocean, yearning for the peace it promised with its deep blue waters.

Squinting her eyes, she tried to imagine England as a dot on the horizon. The island across the North Sea, one of the main players in this horrible war. An island she'd never set foot on, and yet, she betrayed her own country to help them. After what the Nazis had done to her, and her dear friend Rachel, she'd do anything to bring them down.

Even helping the enemy.

Volunteering for the Wehrmacht and becoming a radio operator had been the logical first step to spying for the

British. As soon as she'd arrived in Stavanger, she had been tasked with contacting the local Norwegian resistance cell working with the English. Since then, with German punctuality, she had provided them with the new encryption codes every week like clockwork.

"Let's take a walk along the shore," Gerlinde said and interlaced arms with her. As soon as they'd left the garrison behind, she asked, "Have you heard?"

"Heard what?"

"They're expecting a British invasion from the sea." Gerlinde usually was well informed, beyond what was told to the rank and file. She was a man's woman and had her subtle ways to get more information than she was supposed to have.

"Don't they always?"

"But this time it's in earnest. Haven't you noticed the increased number of soldiers? The garrison is bursting at the seams and they have requisitioned most every building in town."

Lotte raised a brow. "This place has been teeming with soldiers since we arrived."

Gerlinde shook her head. "Not like this. We're preparing for the ultimate victory."

"Ultimate victory?" Lotte stopped to look at her friend. "But for the Allies, not us. This war has been lost since Stalingrad and it's a devilish miracle that it's still dragging on, like a fatally injured soldier refusing to take his last breath."

"Don't say such nonsense. It scares me." Gerlinde pulled her scarf tighter around her as they rounded a corner and were suddenly exposed to the full force of the sea breeze.

Lotte struggled to keep up with Gerlinde's longer stride.

"Why does it scare you? Don't you want the bloodletting to end?"

"I do. But what will become of us, when the enemy wins? Have you heard—"

"Yes, I have heard the rumors. But I'll deal with it when the time comes."

Gerlinde shook her head. "I have no idea how you can be so fatalistic. Aren't you afraid what the enemy will do to you? Torture you? Kill you? Do what they do to women?"

"I don't expect it to be worse than what the Gestapo did to me. They put me in front of a firing squad, remember?" Lotte shuddered at the memory, her stomach flipping over as a wave of nausea threatened to swallow her whole. Only through the intervention of Johann, who'd pulled rank over the Gestapo agent, had she survived. As a result, she owed the man her very life.

"Of course, I remember." Gerlinde scrunched up her nose and quickly changed the topic. Haunted by tragic memories of the past, they both just wanted to forget. "But I'm feeling better with all the soldiers around."

"I'm sure you do." Lotte giggled, causing her friend to shoot her an indignant look. "Although I don't think it'll have much effect. Just look at this coastline; it's much too long and rugged to properly defend. If the British choose to invade, they surely won't land in the Stavanger harbor."

Gerlinde gave her a dark stare and, after a glance at her wristwatch, said, "We have to return to work."

Lotte buried herself in her work and the nostalgic mood passed. Once the shift ended, she and Gerlinde headed over to the mess. Her contact person with the Norwegian resistance, a young woman called Lina, worked in the garrison kitchen.

Usually, Lotte left the code scribbled on a napkin on her tray for Lina to come and collect. The weekly changing code would allow the British to decipher and understand the messages picked up. But today, Lotte glanced around, not finding the young woman anywhere.

A growing disquiet in her gut, Lotte ate as slowly as she could, already feeling Gerlinde's exasperation looming over her. Her friend had caught two handsome young soldiers ogling her and it was clear she wanted to strike up a conversation with them. But since the female auxiliaries and the male soldiers never shared a table in the mess, this wasn't about to happen.

Especially not under the scrutiny of Oberführerin Littmann, who'd made it her personal mission not only to guide the girls during working hours, but also guard their moral integrity during the off hours.

"Are you finally done?" Gerlinde hissed.

"Sorry, but I'm still hungry. Why don't you get up and leave while I go for seconds?" Lotte said, taking pity on her friend.

Gerlinde's eyes narrowed. "Are you sure? I mean, you can always join us later…"

"Go and have fun. I'll be with you in no time at all."

Lotte's anxiety grew as she covertly glanced around the mess hall for Lina. Dread swirled through her chest, but Lotte tamped it down. Lina's absence could have any one of a thousand valid, harmless reasons. It was just that Lotte didn't believe in coincidences or harmless reasons.

Cold sweat formed on her palms at the same time as fear heightened her senses. She couldn't linger much longer at the table without arousing suspicion. For a moment she considered leaving the napkin with the precious codes on the tray for Lina to collect later but realized that would be downright reckless. Shudders of fright ran down her spine as she considered what might happen to her should the codes fall into the wrong hands – should her superiors find out she'd been giving closely held military secrets to the enemy.

An older woman with a white cap and apron approached her, "Can I have this?"

Mouth agape, Lotte stared at her like she was a three-headed monster.

"Your tray. Are you finished? We're closing up," the woman said.

Lotte nodded and in the very moment the woman grabbed the tray she realized her fatal mistake. Stomach churning, she grabbed the traitorous napkin, loudly blew her nose into it and buried the evidence of treason deep down in her pocket to flush it down the toilet at the first possible opportunity.

"I'm sorry." She peered at the woman, wondering whether it would be prudent to ask about Lina's where-abouts. Years earlier, she would have done just that, but she'd learned her lesson the hard way. Gone were the days when she had no compunction and said whatever popped into her head. A demure, intelligent young woman aware of the dangers facing her with every breath she took had emerged in place of the tomboy she used to be.

Finally, curiosity emerged the victor in her internal war.

"Excuse me, I haven't seen you before. There used to be a girl with blond braids attending the mess," Lotte said in as blasé a fashion as she could muster.

"Lina? She's not here anymore." The woman's face took on a mouse-like grimace of fear.

Something was wrong.

Very wrong.

Lotte plastered a tight smile on her face and walked out on legs that had turned to jelly.

Where the hell are you, Lina?

CHAPTER 2

A t this time of year so far up North, days dragged on and on – much longer even than back home in Berlin. When Lotte stepped out of the canteen and into the garrison's yard, the clear blue sky dazzled overhead. After the grueling winter months, when the sun graced the Norwegian coast for a few short hours a day, she marveled at the endless hours of light in late spring.

According to other *Blitzmädel* who'd worked here last summer the sun would never dip beneath the horizon during June and July. Even during the wee hours of the night the world was cast into a dim twilight. Lotte had believed their accounts greatly exaggerated, but alas, it seemed to be true.

She pulled her light coat tightly around her to subdue the shivers running through her body. Fear was shredding her being and she ordered herself to stop being such a coward. *You knew what you were getting into*, she admonished herself. A hundred plausible reasons could be the answer to Lina's mysterious absence from the garrison kitchen.

But one reason lingered.

Attacked Lotte's brain.

Froze the blood in her veins to icicles.

One reason.

Try as she might, she couldn't shake off the foreboding that something had gone wrong. Awfully wrong. The anguish drained her physically and she dragged her feet across the earthen surface in the yard. Suddenly she stopped in her tracks. Her legs felt leaden, her face turned to stone.

"Oh, no! No, no!" She yelled the words but no sound was uttered.

A young woman that looked oddly familiar was being hauled across the yard by military police. Lotte caught a glance of her face. *Lina!*

Run, Lina, run! she silently urged the captive who struggled against the might of three armed men.

Horrified, she watched the uniformed soldiers manhandle the apprehended woman and shove her roughly into a waiting van. Just before one of the men rammed the door closed, Lotte caught Lina's tortured gaze. It was but a split-second, but that expression held eternal sorrow.

An expression that would haunt Lotte for years.

Both women knew what would happen to Lina.

A dizzy spell weakened Lotte's knees, but she couldn't let the panic creeping up her bones gain the upper hand. As much as seeing Lina arrested aroused terror in her, even made her feel physically sick, she simply must keep her cool.

Lotte ducked her head between her shoulders, pulling the collar of her coat up around her ears in a desperate attempt to remain inconspicuous. Her ears burnt with the certainty that any passerby would see the guilt written all over her face. Would at one glance know her true identity. Spy. A traitor to Führer and Fatherland.

One thing was certain. Lina would talk.

Everyone talked. Everyone broke. Eventually.

These men had a range of heinous methods to extract confessions. It was only a matter of time before she spilled the beans about the identity of her contact in the Wehrmacht. Although Lina knew Lotte only by the name of Karla, the Gestapo agents weren't a bunch of stupid old men and would soon connect the dots.

In a reflex, Lotte's legs pushed forward to run, but she caught herself in time and willed her body to remain still – to walk like an innocent woman who had nothing to fear, because she'd done nothing wrong. Somehow Lotte managed to return to her barracks and crawl up the flight of stairs to her room.

Gerlinde was home, singing a popular tune by Zara Leander as she got dressed to go out for a drink, and hopefully, a good time.

"Where have you been?" Gerlinde asked, brushing her hair vigorously.

"Sorry, I got chatted up on the way."

A girlish giggle escaped Gerlinde's lips. "Was he handsome?"

"Why do you always assume it's a man?" Lotte said, half laughing.

"Because of the odds. There are close to a thousand men in the garrison and only two dozen women," Gerlinde responded, and then, bubbly as ever, laid out the evening's plan for Lotte. "Since we don't have to work tomorrow until after noon, I persuaded the old witch to extend our curfew until eleven p.m. Better hurry up and not make us lose precious time."

"I'm not really in the mood to go out tonight." Lotte's entire body still trembled from the impact of what she'd witnessed only minutes ago – and what might follow once Lina talked.

"Come on, it's our only night off this week. We need to have fun once in a while," Gerlinde begged with a pouting mouth. God only knew where she'd procured the red lipstick that she now used to carefully trace her lips. "There's a handsome officer waiting for me."

"Thanks, but no. I've had a terrible day and just want to curl up in bed and sleep for a hundred years." In reality, Lotte was wracking her brain trying to decide whether it was best to make a run for it, or wait for the military police to arrive and take her captive.

"Come on, let's make a night of it. A drink or two will relax you and cheer you up. You're alive! Who knows what tomorrow will bring?" Gerlinde tugged at Lotte's arm. "You can sleep all you want once you're dead."

The exuberant behavior made Lotte giggle and she considered the truth of her friend's words. If she was condemned to die in the near future, she could at least enjoy the little time she had left.

"Well, if that isn't the truth, I don't know what is," Lotte exclaimed as vivid pictures of her last moments on earth whirled menacingly around her mind.

She quickly changed into civilian clothes and added a couple of curls to her forehead. This hairstyle was all the rage these days and it suited her. Unfortunately, she'd run out of makeup and lipstick months ago, but Gerlinde generously loaned her hers.

"Ready to brave the night," she finally said, giving a silly twirl.

"You look gorgeous, sweetheart. And I'm sure my officer will have a dozen of his comrades licking their fingers over you."

"You know that I'm in love with Johann," Lotte objected, tender thoughts about the man who owned her heart sweeping her with nostalgia.

"He's far away, and I can assure you, he'll find relief in the arms of some willing girl, wherever he is now. It's war and the traditional rules about relations have ceased to be valid."

"Not for me. And not for him," Lotte said with a stubborn tone. "We will be faithful to each other."

Gerlinde snorted. "Not even a little kiss?"

"Not even a little kiss." Lotte stood firm. Others might think a kiss was nothing to worry about, but she disagreed.

"Not even if it takes years until you see him again?" Gerlinde teased.

"Not even if it takes my entire life. I will not betray him for as long as he's still alive."

"Oh, girl. But that doesn't forbid a harmless dance with a dashing young officer, right?" Gerlinde grabbed her arm, never one to be serious for too long. They stepped outside, a soft sea breeze rustling the leaves.

"It's so lovely outside," Lotte said, breathing in the sharp fresh air, even as she braced herself for the wrath of her persecutors, who would surely be waiting for her.

"Yes, it is," Gerlinde agreed. "Wouldn't it have been a shame to stay home?"

"As always, you're right, Fräulein Weiler."

"Just listen to me, Fräulein Wagner, and you'll never go wrong." Gerlinde giggled, executing a perfect twirl. "I promise, we'll have a grand time. Anything's possible."

Lotte shuddered at the possibilities of the coming hours and hoped her friend's words didn't prove prophetic.

CHAPTER 3

The two women walked to the town center where their favorite nightspot was located. They stepped into Bar Boca, a lively place frequented by Norwegians and Germans with a great atmosphere, jazz music and dancing. People bent on having a good time despite the war going on outside littered the dimly lit bar.

"This place is packed," Lotte said, struggling to wade through the crowded space. She peered at the patrons, who all had one thing in common: they were intent on unwinding and forgetting everything about the war and the hardships it had brought to the city of Stavanger. Drinks had already numbed the pain and painted wry smiles on the lips of those who wanted to hide their wretchedness.

"The more the merrier," Gerlinde replied happily, never one to be daunted by a room full of attentive men. "Let's see if we can find someone to buy us a drink."

Plenty of German soldiers milled about and Gerlinde seemed to know most of them, acknowledging their wolf whistles and greetings with a shake of her head or a smile, depending on who was the offender.

The two friends threaded their way across the tiny dance floor, where couples were swaying to the rhythm of the lively music. While Gerlinde enjoyed the nearness of gyrating bodies packed so closely together, Lotte fought against a mild form of claustrophobia. She'd learned to dislike masses of people since that fateful day when she was shoved onto a cattle wagon with dozens of other women.

Finally, they arrived at a table occupied by officers from their garrison. But even before Gerlinde could bat her eyelashes at one of them to make him buy their drinks, both of the women were whisked off to dance.

It was all in good fun and Lotte was glad to be invited out of the fog of her dilemma. The young man, Albert, was making a play for her and it was hard not to notice. He was handsome and charming, and Lotte wouldn't have minded his advances if it weren't for Johann. She'd promised him faithfulness when he'd kissed her goodbye in Warsaw six long months ago.

She hadn't seen Johann since, and the last letter she received from him had arrived three months ago. It had been heavily blacked out by the censors and what remained were vague scribbled words that said nothing of his real situation.

Our new cook is much better than the last one. The Ivan is close, but we are confident we'll win. Don't worry about me.

I love you.

Always,

Johann

Shortly after she received the *Feldpost* letter, news broke that Warsaw had fallen. She had no idea whether he'd been ordered out before, had died in action defending the city or… had been captured by the Ivan.

She cast the worry aside and remembered the good times with him. The way he made her laugh… A smile curled her lips. Johann was the last person she should have fallen for. But love didn't ask for convenience or logic, and when Cupid's arrow hit, there was no holding back. She only hoped he'd survive this awful war and would return to her side as soon as it ended. If not, she'd wait. Until the end of the world, if she must.

"You have such a dreamy look on your face. Am I lucky enough to be the reason?" Albert asked, pressing her closer against his chest.

The blood drained from her face and for a moment the guilt swallowed her up. She hadn't done anything, hadn't meant to… and yet, here she was, encouraging this young man.

Casting her eyes downward, she shook her head. "No, I'm sorry. I was thinking of my boyfriend."

"Oh." Albert's jaw fell and he released his grip, holding her with several inches between their bodies. As soon as the song ended, he dropped her hand as if she were a slimy fish and fled from the dance floor.

Lotte glanced around and found Gerlinde sitting at the table with a couple of Germans in officer's uniforms. She passed by the bar and ordered a beer, afraid that something stronger might dampen her senses, and then steered through the crowd to join her friend.

"Alex, where's your suitor?" Gerlinde asked.

"Disappeared as soon as I told him about my sweetheart," Lotte snapped and to her delight she saw the corners of the mouths of some would-be admirers around the table drop. Since she had no patience to fight off unwanted advances she clarified, "Leutnant Johann Hauser is currently in Poland, fighting for the Reich."

Gerlinde shot her a dark stare, followed by a honeyed smile. "Please sit, we were just chatting about the music." Officially jazz music was considered *Negermusik* belonging to an inferior race and therefore prohibited. But here, far away from the Führer's reach, even the younger officers indulged in listening to it, if not with permission of the garrison leaders, then at least with their tacit indifference.

Lotte did as she was asked and sipped on her beer, letting herself relax from the anxiety engulfing her. As time passed, alcohol loosened the tongues of the men at her table and they spoke more frankly than they would otherwise in the garrison.

"The war will soon be over," a dark-haired Leutnant with a Kaiser-Wilhelm- mustache said.

Lotte's spirits soared at hearing this. Usually nobody dared to openly speak such defeatist words for fear of being court martialled. But if this officer openly admitted to it, maybe the war would be over by the time the Gestapo connected the dots and arrested her… It was a tiny straw to hang onto, but it was better than nothing.

"None of this defeatist talk! Germany is invincible!" A zealous Nazi banged his fist on the table. "The war will be over when the Führer says so, and not one day before. Then, we will rule the world and renew it as a better place for the master race."

The mixed group at the table quieted down, until someone changed the topic.

"One of the kitchen aides was arrested today," a young blond man with bright blue eyes remarked casually. "It seems she worked for the Norwegian resistance."

A stunned Lotte turned to stone, barely able to breathe. The fear resting within her woke up with a start and went on a rampage inside her.

"Some people never learn," the Nazi retorted, laughing. "We have disbanded more resistance rings than we care to count. This one won't be the exception. Once our Gestapo friends get her to talk, the rest will be scattering like rats leaving a sinking ship, scrambling to stay alive. An example will be made of this foolish creature."

"She hasn't confessed anything of value so far," the Leutnant said.

"That's because she's been interrogated by amateurs. Just wait and see what the Gestapo will find out," the Nazi laughed. "She will soon be singing at the top of her lungs, eager to rat out her comrades in order to save her worthless skin."

Again, the icy grip of unabated terror whooshed the air out of Lotte's lungs and she struggled to remain calm. The moment Lina talked, Lotte's own life was worth less than a *Pfennig*. Bolting from the bar seemed the sensible thing to do, or better yet, desert and go underground. She had to make a move before it was too late for her to escape. But how?

"You look pale, Alex," Gerlinde said with concern. "Are you alright?"

"Stuffy in here," Lotte replied, hoping to control her

panic and not pass out. "All the cigarette smoke. I feel kind of light-headed... need some fresh air."

"Let's go outside for a while," Gerlinde suggested as Lotte got up to leave.

"You stay here, Gerlinde. I'll be fine once I'm outside. Don't ruin your evening for me. Have a nice time and tell me all about it when you get home."

"No, please stay," her friend insisted. "Let's get some fresh air and something to eat. You'll feel better then."

"Really, I must go."

"You can't go home; the evening's still young."

"No, you certainly can't go home yet, lovely lady," a handsome lad in civilian clothes with the slightest Norwegian accent blocked her way. "Not when we haven't even met."

Before she could protest, he guided her swiftly toward the dance floor.

CHAPTER 4

L otte struggled in the tight grip of the stranger. She was about to kick the impertinent man in the shins when he whispered in her ear. "Would you like a piece of *knekkebrød* with a topping of *leverpostei?*"

She choked on his words, the code phrase for the resistance cell, and had difficulties remembering the appropriate response. Gratefully it took only seconds for the memorized response to kick in.

"I prefer my *knekkebrød* with strawberry jam." She glanced up at him, catching the satisfied grin crossing his face. He had a certain charm that captured her, much like Johann, who wasn't handsome in the traditional sense, but his smile always made her knees go wobbly.

"I'm Harald." He smiled, his strong arms holding her tight against his chest as he led her across the dance floor with masterful and confident strides. He smelled of tobacco and soap.

"A… Karla," she said, catching herself in the last moment.

She breathed in deeply in an attempt to regain her composure.

Harald guided her into the middle of the dancers and held her close, as if they were one. His mastery of the dance made it easy for her to follow the complicated steps. The song ended and he still hadn't spoken another word. He nodded his head in the direction of the band and as if on cue, they played a slow blues number.

He wrapped his arms around her, turning to look at her before he put his cheek against hers as if they were lovers sharing a sweet moment. Despite his brazenness she noticed he had the loveliest blue eyes and so she didn't mind his closeness. Made somewhat heady by the strange effect his unexpected appearance had on her, she was grateful his strong arms held her steady.

"Do you know what has happened to Lina?" she whispered against his ear. He shrugged slightly as if he had no idea what she was talking about. Had she really expected an answer? Wasn't she well aware of the rules that only essential information should be shared? Disappointed at her own oversight, she tried to distance her body from his, but he increased the pressure of his arms around her to keep her plastered against him.

"Have you got the codes?" he whispered, his warm breath teasing her ear.

Lotte had to remind herself that he was here for a reason and *not* to flirt with her, or she would have pushed him away. This man had identified himself as her contact for the codes. Nothing more and nothing less. Or had Lina confessed already, and he'd been sent by the Gestapo to trick her into giving up her secrets? She decided to test him.

"How do I know if you are my contact and not some underground agent sent by the same people who have Lina?"

"You don't. You have to trust that she didn't know the secret code phrase you were given to use in an emergency and thus couldn't betray it." His deep, gravelly voice didn't waver for the slightest moment.

Lotte furrowed her forehead, thinking. It was true. Lina wouldn't know the secret word Lotte had been given in case… it wouldn't make sense. The code was meant for situations exactly like this one, when her first contact was taken out by whatever circumstances. She had to take a leap of faith.

"I don't have them on me right now," Lotte said. "But I can write them down."

"Not here," he murmured into her ear.

She thought for a moment before she came up with an idea. "I'll do it in the bathroom."

"Yes, do that," he agreed and steered them to the corner nearest to the ladies' room. Once the music stopped, he released her from his embrace, saying, "I'll wait for you right here."

The ladies' room was a dimly lit, smelly place and she scrunched up her nose in disgust. The fact that she had to wait for a vacant cubicle added to her misery and a dizzy spell attacked her. She popped her head out of the ladies' room to assure herself that Harald was still waiting for her. She spotted him, surrounded by a trio of giggling girls batting their eyelashes.

She frowned at him, thinking he should keep a low profile. He caught her eye and winked at her and she quickly disappeared behind the door again, just when it was her turn to occupy one of the cubicles.

Already singing victory, it dawned on her that she had neither pen nor paper to write down the codes. But if she stepped out to ask at the bar for what she needed, she'd not only lose the stall, but also be acting suspiciously. Rummaging through her pockets she found a chewed-on stub of a pencil and grabbed some toilet paper. Her heart hammering in her throat, she settled on the toilet lid, disgusting as it was. Her hands trembled so hard she tore the toilet paper to pieces at her first attempt to transcribe the codes.

Lotte uttered a curse and grabbed some more paper. More careful with the fragile material this round, she took her sweet time writing down letter after letter. She squinted her eyes at the work she'd done so far. It wasn't very legible, but would have to do.

Worrying her lower lip, she set out to transcribe the second set of words, when a bang on the door made her jump. With bated breath, her eyes riveted to the door handle, she sat motionless, waiting for Gestapo agents bursting through the door.

"Hurry up, love! I'm about to wet my pants!" a female voice yelled.

Lotte sagged with relief and shouted back, "Just a minute."

"Come on, girl! I've got to go!"

"Sorry! I'll be out in a jiffy!" she promised.

Someone tried to look under the gap in the bottom of the door and she kicked her foot, protesting. "Stop! Give me a moment, will you?"

As soon as she was done, she folded the paper and tucked it up her sleeve. Then she opened the door to a group of women who tried to make a desperate dive into the cubicle. In her hurry to get the secret information to Harald, she forgot to wash her hands, until the disapproving stare of another woman reminded her of the task.

She smiled her apologies and thoroughly washed her hands, trying to be as inconspicuous as possible. But how did one act innocent when the traitorous piece of toilet paper burned holes into her skin?

When she stepped out into the dark hallway next to the dance floor, her courage plummeted. Harald had disappeared.

He wouldn't give up his waiting spot to receive the crucial information for no reason. Something must have happened... Gestapo officers appeared in front of her inner eyes and she couldn't suppress the reflex to raise her hand to her heart. Swallowing down the lump forming in her throat, she finally decided to make her way back to the table where Gerlinde was still going strong.

"What happened to the handsome suitor?" Gerlinde asked, giggling with the abandon of a tipsy mind.

"Stop it," Lotte protested. "Harald's not my suitor. He simply asked me for a dance."

"Oh, Harald, is it?" Gerlinde teased. "Not your sweetheart, eh? You and Harald have sure become best friends in a very short time. But maybe I couldn't see so well from here."

"Probably not, the state you're in." Lotte realized her mistake in disclosing the man's name even if it was a false one. "We should go home. You've had enough."

"Not going home yet. It's our morning off tomorrow," Gerlinde slurred her words and put her arms around Lotte, who had to laugh at her friend. Gerlinde always became quite maudlin after a drink or two.

Lotte, though, felt the anxiety of Harald's disappearance gripping her every cell. The relaxation she'd felt earlier had vanished at the same time he had, and now pure panic swept through her as she tried to keep a smile on her face. She would have left but for the thought that he might still be somewhere in the bar even though she could see no sign of him.

After waiting for a few more minutes, she decided to leave and get rid off the evidence of her treason. But then she saw him, arguing with two German soldiers. Harald's gaze crossed hers, and he quickly glanced away, pretending not to recognize her.

Lotte couldn't hear what they were saying, but the Norwegian seemed belligerent and was soon escorted outside. He went off without the codes, leaving Lotte with them tucked up her sleeve and wondering what to do next.

"Why can't things go smoothly just once?" Lotte cried out in frustration.

"What's wrong?" Gerlinde asked.

"Nothing really," Lotte sighed. "Just thought I'd better make my way home. Gotta work tomorrow."

CHAPTER 5

The day had taken a toll on Lotte and despite the time being barely past ten p.m., exhaustion flooded her system. She would be a total wreck the next day if she didn't grab some shuteye.

People with sharp brains tend to live longer, that's what her brother Richard had used to say when she teased him for sticking his nose into a book instead of jumping into some crazy adventure with her. For once, she hated to admit, he'd been right. She needed all her wits about if she was to come out of this situation unscathed.

Nostalgia attacked her and with it the longing for her family and that precious time before the war shattered their lives and ripped them apart. The very real possibility of dying alone in a country that was not her own hit her square across the chest and she had to hold on to the table to stabilize herself.

"Are you alright?" Gerlinde asked, concern etched into her face.

"Yes, yes, but I should get home." Woodenly, Lotte slipped on her coat and buttoned it up. Right in this moment she had little hope of ever seeing her family again. Not only had Lina been arrested, but also it seemed her new contact Harald had met the same fate.

The only thing she could do was to leave the scene of her crimes and return to the barracks, acting as if nothing had happened and she'd never been a spy for the Tommies.

"Come on, we have forty-five minutes left until we need to be home," Gerlinde said with a disappointed look on her face, as she made to get up and go with her.

"Nonsense, you stay and have fun," Lotte replied. "I'll find my way home, and I'm sure one of the men will see you safely back to the garrison."

Nobody around the table protested, as everyone wanted to make the most of the time until curfew. Gerlinde waved one arm at Lotte and told her, "Sleep well."

"I will," Lotte lied. How could she even pretend to sleep when she feared the military police lurking around every corner? She yearned to leave the crowded bar with its dense fog of cigarette smoke and earsplitting noise. Once outside, the shock of silence and the blast of fresh air revived her spirits. Maybe not all was lost and she would live another day.

The streets were empty, even as the tiniest trace of light illuminated the sky, a foreboding of the endless nights of the North that would begin in less than four weeks. But she had no patience to admire the beauty of the scenery. Instead, she furtively glanced around for Harald, in the irrational hope he might be waiting for her outside.

As she should have expected, he was nowhere in sight.

But neither was the military police. Relief flooded her system, and she took a deep breath of the fresh air coming in from the sea. During the winter time in Stavanger she'd learned to hate the salty, damp air that crept into clothes and bones, making one defenseless against the chill cutting deep into skin and body. But now, in spring, the breeze was a welcome refresher, breathing the hope of better times around every corner.

Everyone knew the war was lost and peace just a stone's throw away. Better times would come, she was sure of it. Just when? Would it be too late for her? She forced the depressing thoughts from her mind, pushed her hands deep into her pockets and sensed the chewed remains of a pencil through the material of the coat. Scorching heat trickled through her as she held onto the suspicious implement, reminding her that the evidence of her treason was still shoved up her left sleeve. In her hurry to flee the bar, she'd forgotten to get rid of it and flush it down the toilet. If anyone found her with the codes there would be hell to pay.

She nervously ducked her head between her shoulders and walked toward the coastline, where the garrison was located, until she heard a low whistle. She stopped to listen, but only the silence of the night echoed back and the distant crashing of waves against the rugged Norwegian coast. Her imagination must be playing tricks on her.

Lotte quickened her pace, balling her hands into fists and huddling them deeper into her coat pockets. Then she heard it again. A distinct whistle. Soft and low, but a definite whistle nonetheless. She stopped again and slowly turned around, scrutinizing the area beyond. A tall person stood hidden in the shadow of one of the houses lining the street.

She hesitated, since she couldn't make out the identity of the person. It might be a trap. Or it might be Harald. Her heart hammered loud enough to block out any other sound and she fought with herself over what to do next. Then, the person stepped out of the shadows and into the moonlight, and she recognized him. Her knees all but buckled and she wanted to scold him for giving her such a fright.

Casually she walked toward his position. Harald didn't speak. He simply reached out and took her elbow, pulling her into the shadows with him. There was no need for subterfuge since nobody was around to witness this charade, but still, he took great care not to be seen during their illicit business of exchanging the codes. And for this, she was grateful.

Wordlessly she handed over the toilet paper and just as silently, he accepted it. A heavy burden fell from her shoulders the moment she saw the grayish piece of paper in his hands. If someone caught them in this instance, it wasn't she who'd be on the hook for her betrayal. From now on it was his mission to keep the evidence from being discovered.

"How will I contact you again?" Lotte asked and felt foolish the moment the words were out.

"Come by the bar every week with the new codes," he replied, looking ahead as if he wanted to bolt. "The bartender you saw today is one of us. He's been instructed."

"Bar Boca?" She looked at him and he shrugged. "So, I'm to hand over the codes to the bartender, not you?" She had to be sure.

"Yes." He led her out of the shadows, but the moment

they emerged, she heard the loud voices of passersby and realized they would be seen. Innocent bar-goers might be the owners of the voices – or military police that patrolled the streets day and night.

Lotte sent a quick prayer of thanks toward heaven that she'd had the foresight to change out of her uniform, because in her civilian clothes she might pass for a regular Norwegian girl walking home with her friend. But a moment of shock later she realized it was well after curfew for the local population and they would no doubt be stopped and interrogated. How should she explain that she was out and about with a Norwegian man at night?

Harald, though, pulled his wits about him like a coat of armor – perhaps he simply had more practice with this kind of situation – and pushed her against the wall, wrapping his strong arms around her and covering her mouth with a passionate kiss.

Her first instinct was to fight his assault, but on second thought she changed her mind. It was the perfect cover for them. Military police wouldn't interrupt kissing lovers, as they had better things to do.

Pressed with her back against the cold wall and her front against Harald's warm body, she glimpsed the street behind his back and saw two German MPs walking toward them. Terrified, she closed her eyes again and found herself responding feverishly to Harald's kiss.

She got caught up so much in the heat of the moment, spurred on by the sheer will to live, that she barely registered the two MPs laughing and offering vulgar advice to the man holding her in his embrace.

The moment the officers moved on without bothering them, Harald broke the kiss and said, "That was close."

It definitely was, much too close for her liking, and in more ways than one. Glad not to have his lips on her anymore, imposing their will on her, a strange sadness ripped through her body at the same time. It had been such an exhilarating sensation to be wrapped up safely in his arms, to feel his warm and strong body pressed against her. To not feel so alone. She could still sense the pressure and taste of his mouth and wondered how to cope with that disconcerting feeling.

"We should get going," Harald said casually, dusting off his jacket vigorously as if he wanted to erase any traces of her. He turned and walked away into the night. No smile, no thank you, no goodnight. What a cad! And what a kisser!

Lotte touched her swollen lips with remorse. She hadn't wanted this kiss, hadn't even asked for it, but much to her dismay, she'd enjoyed it. A kiss from a man who wasn't her dearest Johann. How could she have behaved in such a shameful way? Hadn't they both sworn faithfulness to each other the day she'd stepped onto the train taking her away from him?

The end justifies the means, and I kissed him only to stay alive. Johann would understand. But deep in her heart she feared he might not and decided to bury this little secret in her soul. Along with so many other secrets she carried around, not daring to let any of them ever see the light of day.

CHAPTER 6

Over the next days, Lotte did her best to forget about Lina's arrest, but the debilitating fear accompanied her every waking moment.

On Sunday, Gerlinde convinced her to participate in a trip to the famous rock called Preikestolen overlooking the Lysefjord. Together with a group of male soldiers who organized transport they embarked on the journey to one of the most breathtakingly beautiful spots in all of Norway.

Even Lotte couldn't help but forget about her problems and revel in the serenity of nature as they left the vehicle down on the road and started the two-hour climb up the back side of the rock.

"Isn't this beautiful?" Gerlinde exclaimed, as they walked past lush green meadows, patches with thin forest and deep blue lakes that invited a swim.

Lotte approached the bank and carefully dipped a hand into the water to test the temperature. "Ieeek," she shrieked into the bellowing laughter of her comrades.

Helmut, the soldier who'd organized and driven the vehicle, chuckled, "What did you think? The snowmelt hasn't happened that long ago."

Lotte joined the laughter, deciding that nothing would cloud this wonderful day. Not the war, not her fear, and certainly not the ice-cold water. They chatted wild nonsense while climbing up the moderately steep hill until they finally reached the ledge.

All chatter was silenced in a moment and everyone in their group stood with their jaws hanging agape. It was a sight of supernatural beauty that filled Lotte with awe. Suddenly she, and all humans combined, seemed so small and insignificant against the immense force of nature.

They stood on a rock plateau, around two hundred fifty square feet large, with a vertical drop more than four hundred fifty yards into the blue fjord beneath. On the other side of the fjord she saw the smaller gray rocks topped with green grass and bushes.

But up here, it felt like being suspended in the sky. A soft breeze came in from the sea and the sun shone down on them, warming the stone. Lotte walked as near to the edge as she dared and peeked down, vertigo overtaking her. She swayed slightly and felt a strong hand on her shoulder.

"Careful," Helmut said. "If you want to look down, it's better to lie flat on the stone and crawl up to the ledge.

For a moment she thought he was pulling her leg, but his serious expression changed her mind.

"I'll go with you," he said.

"Alright." Lotte lay on her stomach, the wind rustling the hem of her skirt, and once more she wished women were allowed to wear the much more practical trousers. As soon as her body touched the warm rock, she felt secure. Grounded.

"Better?" Helmut asked her, his face beaming with excitement.

"A lot. Let's go." Together they crawled to the very edge and beyond, until her shoulders were pressed to the ground, but her head hung in the air.

Despite the knowledge that she was safe, couldn't fall, an exhilarating sense of danger, of vertigo rippled through her body, heightening her senses. She'd never before experienced such a feeling of complete weightlessness. She guffawed, and the echo reverberated from the opposite walls of the Lysefjord.

"Watch this," Helmut said and produced a stone the size of his fist from his pocket. He struck out and threw the stone out into the air. Then he counted. "One… two…three..."

"Eleven." The stone dove into the water, leaving a barely visible ring of white ripples, and moments later a soft splashing sound reached their ears.

Lotte was awestruck by the long journey the stone had just completed.

"Eleven seconds," Helmut said, furrowing his forehead in intense thought. "Close to six hundred meters."

Lotte stared at him, not fully following his train of thought. "What did you just do?"

He showed a happy, proud smile and explained, "Just calculating the height. It's really easy. You simply need to divide the gravity acceleration by two and multiply this with the square of eleven seconds' time and you'll get the distance in meters."

"Oh, wow." It didn't seem easy to her to do this kind of challenging calculation, especially not without pen and paper. "How do you know that?"

"Physics first semester. I studied architecture and physics was one of my favorite subjects." His blue-gray eyes darkened with so much nostalgia as he answered, it hit her square in the stomach.

She put her hand on his. "I'm sure you can continue your studies after the war."

"Don't we all wish for that?"

She nodded, his sadness thickening the air to unbearable proportions.

Lotte tried a small smile and thankfully the moment of misery passed and he grinned at her, "At least there'll be lots of work for me as an architect. What gets demolished, must be rebuilt."

They backed away from the edge and looked around to search for the others, who were sitting in the middle of the plateau, admiring the scenery and unpacking the sandwiches they'd brought along.

"What do you want to do after the war?" Helmut asked her as they settled next to the others, opening their own backpacks.

"Me?" She scratched her nose. She'd never given it much thought. "Honestly. I don't know. I never even finished school. It didn't reopen after the summer vacation, because all the boys had been drafted and the girls whisked away for *Reichsarbeitsdienst*." Lotte herself hadn't had to join the compulsory labor service, because she lived on her aunt's farm and all farmhands were exempt. In fact, Aunt Lydia had always requested additional help and she'd regularly received both *Arbeitsmaiden* from the labor bureau and prisoners of war.

When they returned to the garrison in the late afternoon, Lotte felt more relaxed and refreshed than she'd had in months.

"Helferin Wagner, Hauptmann Kochel is expecting you in his office," the sentry greeted her on return.

The fright returned in one swift punch to her stomach, leaving her with wobbly knees. What could the garrison leader possibly want from her? On a Sunday afternoon? There was only one possibility...

Lotte straightened her spine and cast the sentry a small smile. "Thank you. I will quickly change into my uniform and— "

"No, the boss said to send you his way immediately when you showed up."

Another, harder, punch to her stomach. It was a bad sign, if the overly correct Hauptmann Kochel didn't bother with formalities. Suddenly the warm April sun had vanished from her world, leaving her in a bleak and cold cave.

"Th...ank you," she managed to press out between gritted teeth to keep them from chattering. She hurried to the office building and took one deep, but not really calming, breath before she knocked on her superior's door.

"*Herein*," a deep voice said and she entered the office, where the large man sat behind his wooden desk. As was the custom in every official room, a portrait of Hitler hung behind the desk, flanked by two huge Swastika flags. The portrait glared at her with menace, as if the person depicted were alive and the Führer knew that she'd defied him.

Instinctively, she cast her eyes to the ground and shuffled forward.

"Shut the door, please," Hauptmann Kochel said in a clipped tone that conveyed his discomfort at what was to come.

Lotte obeyed his order, prepared for military police to jump out of the corners of the room to arrest her and hand her over to the fearsome Gestapo. Another punch to her stomach that barely allowed her to keep upright.

Out of her mind with anguish, she gratefully collapsed into the chair he indicated. She wanted to bolt. She'd prefer to be shot during escape than be interrogated by the Gestapo thugs and lose her pride along with her life. Nobody could withstand their torture methods, and she racked her brain about whom she would betray when her time came. Lina – a lost cause. Harald? Surely. The bartender? Thankfully she didn't even know his name.

To harness her discordant thoughts, Lotte concentrated on the various emblems on the Hauptmann's uniform. He worked at the harbor of Stavanger but belonged to the army, not the marines. The shoulder straps showed two golden stars.

"Helferin Wagner," he started, steepling his hands meticulously atop the desk. He avoided her eyes and cleared his throat before he continued, "I'm afraid I have bad news for you."

Was that how traitors were informed about their impending arrest? She silently screamed in protest and couldn't keep her hands from flying to her face as if to shield her mind from hearing his devastating words.

"Now, now. Compose yourself, Helferin Wagner," he

said. "We all have to make sacrifices in this war, and I'm the one who has to bring you the sad news that your fiancé, Leutnant Johann Hauser, was taken prisoner by the Soviets near Warsaw."

Despite fear over Johann's situation, she still felt shudders of relief coursing through her body. Her own arrest would have to wait for another day.

"Thank you," she said, even as the news settled into her brain. Her beloved Johann was a captive now. A Russian prisoner of war. That in itself was bad, very bad. Rumors had been running wild and the soldiers had even given a name to the terror a capture by the Ivan evoked: *Russenschreck*. A word whispered with the utmost awe. But at least he wasn't fighting anymore. Out of the line of fire, his chances at survival had grown multifold. Surely they had.

"Is there anything else you might know? His whereabouts? Is he ... wounded?" she asked.

"I'm sorry, but that is all," Hauptmann Kochel replied with an indulgent glimpse at her. "He will remain strong, as will all the other brave Germans who are fighting for our Fatherland. You may leave."

"Thank you, sir." Lotte walked toward the door on unsteady feet. Her hand on the doorknob, she gripped the ice-cold metal in her hand like a lifeline when Kochel said, "Ah, one moment, Helferin Wagner, there's another matter..."

This is it. I'm done for.

The terror returned to her bones faster than a Stuka bomber swooped from the sky. She turned to look at her superior. "Yes?"

"The Norwegian girl who worked in the kitchen... Lina, I

believe was her name." The words slowly slipped from his mouth and he must have observed the color leaving her face.

"Are you alright, Fräulein?" he asked. "You look very pale."

"My fiancé." She put her hand over her mouth. "I'm sorry, sir. I can't bear to think of him suffering."

"Please don't assume he is suffering. I say the chap is damn lucky. As a prisoner he will be out of the rain and hail of bullets. We must have faith and hope for the best," he said gruffly. "Now about this kitchen aide. You know her, don't you?"

"Everyone knows her. She's been serving in the mess since I arrived here," Lotte said vaguely.

"She's been arrested."

"Arrested? Why?" Lotte feigned ignorance.

"You did not know about her arrest?"

"No, sir. I… I wondered why she hadn't been at the canteen this past week, but it never occurred to me… she was merely a local kitchen aide. Not someone I would socialize with."

"So, you weren't friendly with her?" he said, a sharp attentiveness in his eyes.

"No."

"And yet you asked for her at the mess the other day." He raised his eyebrow quizzically. "What was all that about?"

"That? I…" She desperately thought for a viable reason. "…I believe I asked about her whereabouts because it seemed strange to me she wouldn't be on duty that day." A glimpse into his eyes showed her that he wasn't convinced.

"Alright, I'll admit it. I had a sore throat and wanted to ask her to make me some hot soup to take back to my quarters."

His lips pursed with disapproval. "Why her and not some other kitchen personnel?"

"I'm so sorry." Lotte pressed out some tears for effect. "I know this is forbidden and... I really don't want to get her into trouble for it... but last December when I was down with a bad cold, she brought hot soup to my quarters. Please, don't punish her for her kind heart."

Hauptmann Kochel's face relaxed somewhat. "Rules are there for a reason. Even if you don't understand why it's forbidden to take food from the canteen to your quarters, but..." He gave her a scrutinizing stare that caused a slice of fear to stab her in the chest. "But bringing you soup is the least of Lina's problems. She will be punished for a much more severe crime."

Lotte's mouth hung agape. "A crime? Oh God, did she murder someone?"

He reared back, his chair creaking underneath his weight. "What makes you think so? Does she look to you like someone who could commit such a heinous crime?"

"Oh no... I... I don't know... because you said a severe crime," Lotte stuttered. She was getting caught in her own cobweb of lies and pretenses.

"This ungrateful woman worked for the Norwegian resistance." Kochel slammed his fist onto the desk with such force that Lotte jumped.

CHAPTER 7

"Did you know about that?" Kochel's eyes bored into her brain as if to uncover a secret connection between the two women. "Did you know that the kind-hearted woman who helped you to break garrison rules was involved in subversive activities?"

"No... how could I even imagine that?" Lotte murmured. She didn't have to fake the blood draining from her face and the sudden dizziness she experienced. "I'm shocked. I had no idea!"

"Of course you didn't know," her superior said sarcastically.

Lotte struggled to keep her hands from trembling. "How can such a nice girl do something so awful? I find these accusations very hard to believe. Hopefully the truth will come out."

"No doubt, the truth will soon be discovered, Helferin Wagner," he said with a sardonic smile on his face. "And I doubt it will set her free. Our people don't make mistakes. In fact, it will implicate other enemies of our Reich. "

"You're right, sir," Lotte said with feigned contrition. The Hauptmann might be one of the Gestapo informers, hidden in plain sight. People were browbeaten by the Nazi propaganda of fear, whose far-reaching tentacles permeated the public like a virus. Even people as high up in the military hierarchy as Kochel weren't immune. She decided to lay it on thick. "In spite of the obstacles, the Party is doing a splendid job."

"A magnificent job!" He couldn't resist the flattery, although she wondered how much of it was honest and how much was playing to the house the way she did. "Norwegians can now see the benefits of Nazism. They see how much their country has improved after German occupation. People go to their ordinary jobs and children go to school. They work on German construction projects, while their companies get work from the Germans. Everyone is prosperous and happy. Soon we will leave the transition phase behind and form one superior Aryan race to rule the world."

They don't enjoy freedom, though. But who cared about individual freedom in the face of world domination? Certainly not the Party.

He also failed to mention that Norwegian leaders, civilians and other officers were removed if they didn't do what the new order wanted them to. Much had been destroyed. Buildings, factories and entire towns were bombed and burnt to the ground. Food, clothing and other goods were in short supply and rationed. People experienced a difficult time and the future looked uncertain.

"Is there anything I can do to help the investigation?" she

asked, in an attempt to interrupt his paean to the Nazi ideology.

"That despicable woman has been sent to the Gestapo for deep interrogation, even as we speak," he said cheerfully. "She will soon sing brighter than a nightingale."

The impact of his statement almost knocked her out. She felt its sharpness cutting into her flesh as if they were knives instead of words. She knew full well what deep interrogation meant. It had very little to do with talking.

Swallowing down the bile in her mouth, she clasped her hands to doorknob, until her knuckles became white as freshly fallen snow. Mercifully, someone knocked at the office door, interrupting her train of thought.

"*Herein!*" Kochel called out and she opened the door. In came a very distraught-looking soldier.

"Sir, I'm very sorry to disturb you, but…" the soldier wriggled like a snake in captivity and Lotte wondered what kind of bad news he'd been tasked to deliver, "…this woman, Lina… she has killed herself."

"How on earth could this happen?" the Hauptmann exploded upon hearing the news even as another wave of blessed relief coursed through Lotte's veins at the demise of another. "Am I cursed having to serve with a bunch of incompetent fools?"

The messenger didn't get a chance to reply.

"Who was responsible for this? Do you know what the Gestapo will think about us? Not even capable of keeping one damn female prisoner alive! I swear, heads will roll for this. And it won't be mine!" Hauptmann Kochel's face had turned beet-red and Lotte pressed her body against the wall, hoping he might forget her presence.

"I'm… just… the messenger," the frightened soldier stammered, apparently afraid he'd personally be tried for incompetence, collusion and possibly treason.

"Off you go, Wagner!" Kochel bellowed at Lotte. Her heart beat like a drum as she darted through the door into the silent hallway.

She didn't look back until she arrived at her quarters, where she flopped down onto her bed, torn apart by violent emotions. Despite the awful news of Lina's suicide, it also gave her a sense of relief, immediately followed by sharp pangs of guilt, easing into gratefulness. Lina had done the one thing she knew would prevent her from betraying her friends – including Lotte. Although Lotte was barely a friend, not even an acquaintance, just someone who'd relayed secret information to her. A co-conspirator against the Third Reich.

Sadness engulfed Lotte. A young, vibrant woman had made the ultimate sacrifice to rescue the cause. Another life wasted. But then, what wasn't a waste in this godawful war? Millions had died already and millions more would die, if the Allies didn't put an end to this soon.

Despite Hauptmann Kochel's pep-talk, Lotte knew that even he and his higher-ups believed the war was lost. There was no chance in hell the Wehrmacht could turn this around, as campaign after campaign of experienced, but worn out and war tired, German soldiers crumpled under the onslaught of fresh troops from the Allies. On top of those, the men of each liberated country took up arms to fight together with the Allies against the bedeviled Nazis. And who could blame them?

Not Lotte.

Once her heart stopped racing, worry about Johann attacked her. What had the Russians in store for him? How would he be treated? The disturbing news about both him and Lina on top of the tension she'd been living with for the past week overwhelmed her, and she succumbed to it, sobbing desperately into her pillow.

Much later, Gerlinde whooshed into the room, still exhilarated from their trip to the Lysefjord.

She stopped in her tracks, staring at Lotte. "What's wrong?"

"It's… Johann. He's been taken prisoner," Lotte sobbed.

Gerlinde's expression reflected the impact of the news, but she kept her voice even as she said, "I'm sorry. But it could be worse. Don't you think? He could be wounded or dead."

Lotte sniffed, blinking away a tear. "I know. But I can't bear to think of what he might be going through."

Everyone had heard the propaganda about the *Russenschreck.* No doubt, Goebbels and his propaganda ministry exploited the fear to keep the soldiers fighting until the last drop of blood. But Lotte was convinced there must be some truth to it.

"Don't believe all you hear," Gerlinde suggested. "Prisoners of war have to be treated according to the Geneva Convention."

"Only that… the Soviet Union never signed it." Lotte's sobbing intensified and Gerlinde sat down by her side, holding her in her arms like a baby. Lotte felt the comfort of a friendly soul and was reminded of the times her mother had done the same, when she was still a child.

"I'm sure you'll soon get a letter from him and he'll tell you that he's alright and you have no reason to worry."

"The letters will be censored," Lotte moaned.

Gerlinde softly reproached her friend. "You should be grateful he is no longer on the battlefield and out of the line of fire."

Despite her desperation, Lotte had to laugh. "That's exactly what Hauptmann Kochel said."

"See? When even the boss says so, it must be true. Be brave, I'm sure you and Johann will be reunited as soon as this war ends. Which is more than I can say for myself."

In contrast to Lotte, who wanted to do her bit for the war effort – although in a very different way than the recruiters for female auxiliaries would dare to imagine – Gerlinde had joined up out of boredom. Living the privileged life of a great landowner's daughter in East Prussia, she'd grown tired of being confined to her golden cage and had sought adventure. By now, though, she regretted her decision dearly and would rather have stayed with her family.

"Have you had news from your family?" Lotte asked.

"Not since the letter I got last month." A steep frown appeared on Gerlinde's forehead, betraying her worry for her family.

"I'm sorry." Lotte thought back to the contents of that letter. Gerlinde's family had written her that they'd decided to flee from the Red Army in January, across the frozen *Haff*. Shudders ran down her spine at the thought of having to step on the treacherous ice of the Baltic Sea while being chased by the Red Army on the ground and strafed from the air.

"My poor mother." Gerlinde's gaze became distant, as if her soul was flying across the lands to be with her family and she murmured unconsciously, "I don't even know if they made it across, or where they are now. Even the image of seeing them sinking into the deadly icy waters… fighting for breath…" Her hand flew to her chest and Lotte squeezed her hard.

Both women sat, pressed against one another, hanging on to their morbid thoughts, each one of them fearing for those she loved most. Finally, Lotte gathered her wits and said, "Your family is probably in a safe place by now. And we shouldn't dwell on dreadful thoughts, as it won't help anyone."

CHAPTER 8

The next day, Lotte went to work as usual. A certain tension hung in the air, but nothing she could point her finger at. Everyone in the garrison seemed to be jumpy and an unusual amount of activity took place.

Lotte wondered if it had to do with Lina's suicide and the impending investigation. No doubt, someone had to suffer the consequences for letting an important witness die on their watch.

"Wonder what's going on," Gerlinde said. "It's like a bunch of school boys going on an excursion."

"Maybe they are. Have you noticed the absence of supervisors today?"

"You don't... we're not... do you think they're abandoning the garrison?" Gerlinde whispered.

"No idea. I wish they would, because that would mean..."

"...the war is all but over."

Lina came to her mind and Lotte became all agitated.

She had to inform the resistance cell about the girl's death. It might help to save another life, frightfully awaiting being discovered.

"Let's go into town after work," Lotte suggested.

"Great idea," Gerlinde eagerly agreed, never one to dwell long on dreadful thoughts. "Spend our pay on traditional Norwegian food."

"If there is any," Lotte said, laughing. Although she knew there was always food to be had for a German in uniform. "That reminds me that I left my silk scarf at Bar Boca – the one my sister Ursula gave me – I must get it back. We could stop there on our way back."

"Aha! It's that tall, handsome guy you met, isn't it?" her friend teased. "Anything I should know about?"

"Nonsense. He disappeared the moment the song ended," she scoffed to show her disinterest. "Seriously, that scarf is precious to me. I'd hate to lose it. Just a quick word with the bartender; you can even wait outside if you don't want to go in."

"Yes sir," Gerlinde agreed with a mock salute and the girls giggled, forgetting themselves for a while. They walked the half-mile into town, admiring the wooden houses painted in pastel colors. The narrow streets curved elegantly between the quaint houses. Coastal artillery dotted the rugged seaboard, clearly visible against the horizon. It served as a constant reminder of the war raging on, even though they didn't notice much of it, here at the far end of Norway, where the European continent met the roughness of the untamable North Sea.

The laughter of children playing drew Lotte's attention. It was their disregard of their environs that touched her deep in her heart. They enjoyed their games without a care for the anti-aircraft batteries, tanks and artillery forces that were ready to take on an invasion.

As they strolled along the cobbled streets, Gerlinde said, "Did you hear about that girl from the kitchen? Caught for being a resister. Killed herself to evade just punishment."

"Oh, please don't remind me about that," Lotte shot back, her body rigid with tension. "It's all too depressing."

"Yes, very sad," her friend continued thoughtlessly. "How bad she must have felt to kill herself rather than face the Gestapo."

"Please stop. I mean it," Lotte begged. "I saw Lina around the canteen, even said hello to her a couple of times. She was so young and sweet, may her soul rest in peace. Let's talk of happy things – like what we want to do once the war is over."

"First thing, I'll find my family and return with them to our lands."

Lotte doubted that returning to that part of East Prussia would be a viable option. It had become an enclave and a thorn in Stalin's side after big parts of the area had been ceded to Poland at the end of the Great War. He surely wouldn't give it back. But she kept her mouth shut and nodded to the reminiscent nostalgia coming from her friend.

"Sorry, we're still closed," the barkeeper called out as she opened the door and stepped into the twilight. As soon as he saw her uniform, he changed his demeanor and said,

"Although, if you want an early drink, I could make an exception for you."

She glanced around the empty place that looked so different now than the other day when it was bursting at the seams with bodies eager to forget. For her purpose it served even better not to have any other patrons present.

"No thanks, I was actually looking for my scarf," she said, quickly crossing the dance floor until she came to stand right in front of the bartender.

"Sorry, no scarf was found." He peered at her suspiciously.

She bent across the bar. "Are you sure?" and then on a whisper, "Lina killed herself, before…" The rest of her sentence lingered unspoken in the air, but judging by the glimmer in the bartender's eyes, he knew that she'd come to reassure him.

He pretended to do some searching, to fool anyone who might be looking, although there was nobody around. "No, Fräulein, no scarf here." Lowering his voice, he added, "Don't come back." With those words he turned his back on her and busied himself organizing his mixers.

"Did you get your scarf?" Gerlinde asked, as Lotte returned to her friend waiting outside.

"No," she replied dejectedly. "I'm afraid someone has found it useful."

"Don't fret, Alex. It's getting warmer by the day; you won't need it for a long time."

"That's a relief," she said with a sarcastic tone.

Gerlinde must have misunderstood Lotte's curt answer, because she touched her friend's shoulder gently. "It's been a hard time – for all of us. You will see Ursula soon and then you don't need the scarf to remind yourself of her."

"I don't know what I would do without you." A wave of gratitude warmed her heart. Without Gerlinde's friendship all of this would have been so much harder.

CHAPTER 9

The days dragged on and Lotte relaxed – a bit. With every passing moment, the threat of the Gestapo arresting her faded. If Lina had talked before she killed herself, they'd have acted already. Whispers about the last days of the war were everywhere, but even that didn't make her smile. The grief over the senseless death of the young woman prevented real joy. Because it just as easily could have been her cold and in the ground.

All throughout the garrison and beyond, rumors were rife, and confusion was the order of the day. Lotte and Gerlinde kept going to the radio room every day for their shift, but even the messages they received and sent became increasingly chaotic.

"Something big is happening, I just wished we knew what," Lotte said.

"Have you seen that files and equipment are being packed and trucks keep coming and going?" Gerlinde replied.

"I sure did. Fingers crossed that it's good news and we'll soon be home again." Another message came in and Lotte interrupted the conversation, transcribing the dits and dahs. "Can't make sense of it," she murmured and showed it to her friend.

"That's because it's double encrypted. We have to give it to the boss and he'll have someone else decrypt it for him."

Lotte glanced at her friend, unsure whether she was joking or not, since this had never happened before.

"Come on," Gerlinde laughed. "Don't tell me you didn't know this. It's somewhere back in the rulebook. I had it happen only once before."

"And that was when?"

"Before you came to Warsaw. We later learned the message had announced the landing in Normandy."

A shudder wracked Lotte's body. "Does that mean… the Allies are going to land in Norway?"

"We don't know. But it could be. In any case the message is super important and we'd better inform the boss right away." Gerlinde took the paper from her hands and rushed into the next room, where their supervisor had his office.

Sitting on pins and needles, Lotte barely managed to write down the flurry of messages coming through the ether until Gerlinde returned and helped out.

"And?" Lotte finally asked, when their shift ended.

"And what?"

"What did the message say?"

Gerlinde laughed out loud. "You didn't expect him to read it out loud in front of me, now did you?"

"Of course not." A wave of hot embarrassment flowed over Lotte at her own lack of sense.

Another day passed and the tension at the garrison was increasing in the same rhythm as Lotte's curiosity. But no news was given and no one in the ranks had the slightest idea of what was going to happen next.

Then suddenly, Oberführerin Littmann, who was in charge of all the female auxiliaries, independent of their line of duty, gathered them and said, "Pack your things and assemble in the courtyard one hour from now. All *Wehrmachtshelferinnen* are evacuated back to the Reich. Immediately."

"It's finally happening," Lotte said as two dozen women hurried to their barracks to pack their belongings.

"We're going home, Alex!" Gerlinde couldn't help doing a little dance.

"Five minutes to evacuation," Oberführerin Littmann shouted as she stood by the truck, checking woman after woman off her list.

Lotte climbed onto the bed of the truck and found a place near the solid side, that reached almost to her hips. Hoops took the canvas covering that was latched to the solid sides. As more women squeezed inside like sardines into a tin, she had to bend her knees, and wrapped her arms around them.

"Hey! Look where you step," someone yelled and a ripple of moving bodies claimed the truck.

Lotte huddled deeper into the corner, keeping her suitcase between her legs. Gerlinde sat beside her, adopting the same fetal position.

"Does anyone know where we are going?" someone asked, but nobody knew the answer. *Home.* That was what everyone hoped. There wasn't a woman in the truck who wasn't sick and tired of the war and just wanted to go home.

Despite the comfortable position in Norway, where the battlegrounds were hundreds of miles away, they all longed to return to their families – hoping against hope there'd be someone to come back to.

At last, Oberführerin Littmann came and announced, "We're driving to Kristiansand and from there a ferry will cross us over into Denmark." Before anyone could ask a question, she pulled down the flap and latched it onto the tailgate. Then she climbed into the driver's cab. As soon as Lotte heard the door slam shut, the truck set into motion.

"Looks like we have quite the journey ahead," Gerlinde murmured. "About three hundred miles give or take. That is if we take the direct route."

"How do you know?" another woman asked.

"Gerlinde spends her leisure time plastered in front of the huge map hanging at the wall in the radio room," Lotte explained. "She has memorized all the countries in Europe, including their main cities and distances between them. She can also tell you the exact location of all the garrisons in Norway and where the cutest soldiers live."

Laughter burst out in the crammed vehicle and took away some of the tension. Lotte tried to relax and get some shuteye, but it was a futile effort. Their assigned driver must be a true maniac, because he sped along the damaged roads and didn't even bother to evade the inevitable potholes.

At times the heavy truck jumped up and down like a rubber boat at sea, tossed about by the waves. "Ouch, "she yelled, as her head banged against the metal structure.

Hours later Lotte's behind became numb, but she

couldn't move, because every inch of floor was covered with human limbs or suitcases. It was dark inside the truck and despite the awful rumbling, Lotte must have dozed off. She woke from bright light hitting her face when the back flap was opened, every bone in her body aching.

"Out, out, girls," Oberführerin Littmann ordered the disoriented group of entangled limbs.

It took some time to sort out legs, arms and suitcases, but finally woman after woman stood on stiff legs, jumping down from the truck onto a patch of sand.

A sign read "Kristiansand Harbor", and even before leaving the vehicle, Lotte smelled the familiar scent of salt water and heard the deep horn of a big ship. She ventured out on her numb legs, which were now pricked with needles as the blood shot back into them.

Still, she was glad to get out of the truck. The darkness and the oppressiveness of being locked inside had reminded her of awful times in Warsaw. Back then… when she'd first met Johann.

The thought of him warmed her heart. Sadness followed the warm sensation, chasing it away. What was he enduring right now? When would she see him again? Where would she even look for him?

"Come on." Gerlinde knocked her elbow into Lotte's ribs and handed her their two suitcases, before she climbed from the truck. "I'm glad to step out of that stinking thing."

Some of the women were in an apparent hurry to relieve themselves after endless hours of driving, and Lotte saw them disappear behind the bushes.

"I could do with something to eat," she said.

Oberführerin Littmann must have heard her, because

she gave her a stern glance and said, "You'll have to wait until we board ship – like everyone else."

"Yes, ma'am." Long ago, Lotte had learned that in the Wehrmacht it didn't do any good to protest, complain or object.

The Oberführerin counted her group, and then led the girls down to the harbor. Although the sun blazed overhead, dark gray thunderheads loomed in the distance. The group stopped near a vessel that had been requisitioned for troop transports and watched the loading of dozens of military vehicles, tanks, howitzers, mortars on wheels and other peculiar objects.

Someone approached their group, putting their names on a list and handing out sandwiches and water to every woman. Lotte bit into her sandwich with abandon. Several companies of soldiers stood around, smoking cigarettes and launching salacious remarks at the women.

"Look, a bunch of Blitzmädel, we're in for a treat," one of them said.

"Softest mattress ever," another one answered with a bawdy smirk on his face.

"We really oughta get some action in the sack... those Norwegian girls are prudes like none other."

"Maybe with you..."

Lotte deliberately blocked out their offensive talk and focused on the deep blue water in the harbor. She had never been on such a vessel and a slight queasiness took hold of her. So far her only experiences with floating contraptions had been an air mattress, a rowing boat on one of Berlin's lakes and the short ferry rides between the Danish islands. But this ferry was a whole different story.

The dark clouds had overtaken most of the sky, blocking out the sun and the wind howled around the harbor buildings. Huge waves rolled in from the sea and crashed against the jetty with such force Lotte thought the rocks might break. In Stavanger she'd always enjoyed the dramatic spectacle – from the safety of the shore. But now, as she was supposed to set foot on one of the cockleshells tossed about by the angry waters, she couldn't find any beauty in the crashing waves.

Gawking seagulls flew across the harbor nosediving into the water for whatever they deemed edible. Lotte squinted her eyes into the distance, but couldn't make out land. She knew it was only a hundred sea miles across the Skagerrak Strait to Denmark, but as far as she was concerned, it could have been a thousand sea miles across the Atlantic Ocean. What difference did it make if they were shipwrecked ten, a hundred or a thousand miles from land? And suffer a shipwreck they would, she was sure of it. The white froth of the waves had reached the height of the solitary beacon standing at the far end of the jetty.

Oberführerin Littmann discussed something at length with the officer in charge of boarding the troops, but finally she returned to the women and said, "All set. We can board now. The ship will sail under cover of night and we should arrive in Denmark in the morning."

"How will they even know where to sail by night?" Lotte whispered.

"They navigate with compass and sextant, stupid," a girl from the Luftwaffe meteorological service explained. "It's much like the airplanes do. The only problem comes when there's no clear sky, because you can't properly dead-reckon your position."

"Oh, thanks," Lotte said, unsure whether that should ease her discomfort or not. Those dark clouds looming overhead made her mighty nervous, even more now that she knew the captain needed clear skies to steer his ship.

"Won't those waves damage the ship?" another woman asked.

One of the soldiers had overheard them. "Of course not. These vessels are built for worse than that. No reason to chicken out. Although I can offer my reassuring embrace to any one of you who is afraid."

"Of course he will," Gerlinde whispered. "Hoping to get a free pass."

"Not your type?" Lotte teased her, gaining an indignant glance.

"Hurry up. The ship won't wait for us," the Oberführerin admonished them.

Lotte grabbed her suitcase and crossed the swaying gangway, her gaze glued to the ship's railing. Usually, she loved water, was a good swimmer, but the gurgling blue-black waters beneath her didn't look inviting. It was an irrational fear, but for some reason she already saw herself struggling to keep afloat, her uniform with the bulky shoes dragging her down, deep into the waters.

"There's nothing to worry about," she heard a familiar voice through the fog that thickened her brain, but she could only shake her head. There was, in fact, a lot to worry about.

Gerlinde must have lost her patience and grabbed

Lotte's hand, pulling her across the gangway onto the heaving ship. "I didn't know you were afraid of the sea."

"I didn't know myself," Lotte heard her own distorted voice saying. Clasping her suitcase with one hand and Gerlinde's arm with the other one, she followed her friend. Gerlinde found a sheltered spot for them to sit on deck and Lotte narrowed her eyes at the retreating shoreline with its distinctive rocks and hills and wooden houses.

"So, that's the end of our time in Norway," she mumbled, imprinting the memories in her brain.

"I guess it is," Gerlinde remarked with a deep sadness in her voice.

Lotte knew her friend worried about the uncertain fate of her family, and she put her arm around Gerlinde's shoulder. Together they would make it across the sea, and back home.

The unsteady craft pounded and rolled, breasting the oncoming waves, as it navigated the rough waters of the Skagerrak Strait. After a while, Lotte got used to the movement and thought it wasn't all that bad. But her reprieve only lasted until the ship changed course and the waves hit the hull sideways, making it tilt over from side to side.

Vomit rising in her throat, all she could do was rush to the railing and bend over, retching. She continued to feed the fish until nothing but green bile came out. Only then did she venture a glance at both sides, her eyes verifying what her ears and nose had surmised: rows of men and women lined the railings, losing the contents of their stomachs. Too weak to move, she clung to the railing, hoping this journey would end before she died.

Once again, Gerlinde came to her rescue. "It gets better when you lie down."

Indifferent to everything, Lotte followed her friend back to their sheltered places and didn't protest when Gerlinde ordered her to lie down. It might be slightly better, or it might not. Lotte did not know and did not care. All she wanted was for this awful seasickness to end – whether that happened because they reached land or she died, she didn't prefer one over the other right now.

CHAPTER 10

Lotte's first sight of Denmark was the little fishing village of Hirtshals. But she would have disembarked from the ship anywhere, if only she could leave behind the rolling, jumping, and tilting monster. In her hurry to get off the vessel, she squeezed through the onslaught of military vehicles disembarking and didn't look back until she reached the terra firma of the jetty.

As soon as she sensed land beneath her feet, the nausea dissolved in an instant as if it had never existed. Only her hungry stomach reminded her of the emptiness inside.

"Thank goodness we survived this trip through hell," she said.

"Now you're exaggerating. It wasn't even a real storm," one of the few women who hadn't become seasick said.

"Well, if that was just a minor wind, I don't want to experience a full-grown storm." Lotte searched for a place to shelter, because the rain was coming down in buckets and her soaked uniform didn't put up much resistance to the scathingly chilly wind.

Half an hour later, every vehicle had been unloaded and the ferry sailed away to collect another load. The soldiers had left with their companies, leaving the Wehrmachtshelferinnen alone, seemingly abandoned like castaways marooned on a desert island.

"How bleak this place is," Gerlinde said, standing in the chilly waiting area at the harbor. The women around her agreed.

"It's the weather that's ugly," Lotte added. "I'll bet it's lovely when the sun shines." Her comment didn't inspire cheer; instead glum faces expressed annoyance at Denmark's hostile welcome.

"What are we supposed to do here anyway?" a blackhaired young woman complained softly.

Oberführerin Littmann had been rushing up and down talking to every officer she could engage, to no avail. She finally returned to her girls and said, "Apparently nobody was advised of our arrival."

None of them dared say a word, but the women looked at each other and Lotte saw her own thoughts mirrored in their eyes. What the Oberführerin had told them wasn't the truth. More than one of the women had overheard snippets of talk and it was clear that the supreme commander in Denmark, General Georg Lindemann, had adamantly opposed any evacuation of troops, even female auxiliaries. About a week ago he'd announced that he would defend Denmark against every attack, from whichever side, to the last bullet and the last breath.

He considered the presence of the evacuated female

auxiliaries a nuisance, even a hindrance to his continued war efforts. Their showing up here reminded the soldiers under his command that others had stopped the fighting already. Lotte suspected that the awful welcome they'd be given in General Lindemann's region might be a statement to show that he, indeed, wanted to fight until the last man.

"It looks like we'll have to wait here until the garrison command can send us transport," the Oberführerin said. Lotte almost pitied her for her unfortunate role in this badly planned evacuation that had become a political statement. The older woman might be strict, even pedantic at times, but she always had the well-being of her charges in mind.

Morning turned into afternoon and Lotte's stomach grumbled with fury. The prior day's sandwich she'd turned over to the fish, and now her body demanded food. But there was nothing edible to be had, not even water, except for the rain still pouring down by the bucket load.

After another hour, drenched and shivering, she sat down on her shabby, wet suitcase. She crouched and hugged her knees tightly, burying her face in her sodden scarf. Most of the other women followed suit. It was a weary band of females, resembling drowned rats.

"Can't we walk to the garrison?" the black-haired girl asked.

Oberführerin Littmann only shook her head. Perhaps it was too far, or perhaps she had no idea where it was. Smaller ships landed and sailed, military vehicles dashed past them, locals gave them suspicious, disdainful or pitying glances. And just when Lotte was resigned to spending the night in this hostile place, a truck drove up and stopped right in front of them.

A young soldier hopped out, his blond shock of hair peeking out from under his tin helmet. "You the stranded Blitzmädels? Hop on!"

On any other occasion, Oberführerin Littmann would chastise him for the disrespectful manners. Today though, she was apparently too delighted to finally receive the transport they'd been waiting for all day and let it slide.

"Get up and board the truck," she ordered her girls.

The journey took the better part of an hour, but finally they arrived at a garrison that seemed to be stuck in time.

Every last soldier was fully armed, awaiting the final proper battle of the war – despite the knowledge that the war was already lost and it was only a matter of time until the Allies arrived in Denmark.

"Oh well," Gerlinde sighed, too tired to say anything else.

If the girls had wished for proper barracks with a wash-room just for them, they were disappointed. They were crammed into a concrete building that probably had served as a meeting room before someone had hastily equipped it with blankets and bed sheets.

The wind whistled through the broken windowpanes into the drafty room. There was no heating and Lotte hoped the rain would stop sooner rather than later, or they'd all catch a cold in their wet clothes.

"You are allowed to dress in civvies, until we dry your uniforms," the Oberführerin said.

"What's happened to the dragon? That's against the rules," Gerlinde said with mock indignation.

"She's as pissed as we are about the horrible treatment. I

guess that's her way of rebelling," Lotte answered, peeling out of the wet clothes and rummaging through her suitcase for something warm to wear. No sooner had the women changed into dry clothes than someone knocked on the door announcing they could go to the mess and get food.

Since General Lindemann was prepared to fight the ultimate battle of the war, there was no further talk of getting the women to Germany. For the time being, it seemed, they were stuck in their makeshift barracks, bored to death, waiting to be the witnesses of his military glory.

"You never told me what exactly you were doing before the war, Gerlinde," Lotte asked her friend.

"Me? Not much." Gerlinde smiled as she dove deep into her memory. "I was the typical spoiled brat. My father owned vast lands in East Prussia and my mother often jokingly said that it was a day's travel to visit our closest neighbors."

Lotte couldn't fathom how it must have been like to grow up in the country far away from any kind of civilization. She herself had grown up in a small two-bedroom apartment together with her parents, her brother Richard and her two older sisters Anna and Ursula. She sighed.

"Hey, what's that? Thinking about Johann again?"

"No, about my family. My father has been in Russian captivity for years now."

"I thought you were orphaned?" Gerlinde squinted her eyes at her.

Lotte's mouth snapped shut. For a moment she'd forgotten about her cover story. Alexandra Wagner was a single child. A single and *orphaned* child. "I am, why?"

"Because you said your father is a Russian POW."

"Surely not. I said my uncle is a Russian POW. And I really need to go to the toilet now." Lotte shot up and rushed out of the building. She had to be careful and stick to her cover story at all times. Charlotte Klausen was dead – she perished at the hands of the Nazis in the Ravensbrück concentration camp.

Outside, she walked around the courtyard, inhaling the night air that smelled of spring. In a few days it would be May. One year ago she'd last seen her oldest sister Ursula. Ursula had stopped working as a prison guard after giving birth to her daughter Eveline and now helped out Aunt Lydia on her farm in the south of Germany.

Mutter, though, had not been allowed to leave Berlin. Her *womanpower* was needed for the war industry, where women had all but replaced the men. She had looked old when Lotte had visited her on furlough last November. Old, tired and hopeless.

Lotte had felt rather guilty, because she'd visited her mother only once during her furlough. Anna, her second sister, had decided it was best when nobody saw them together, especially not their overly nosy neighbor, Frau Weber. That vicious gossip would have nothing better to do than run to the police telling them she'd seen someone looking just like her neighbor's late daughter.

I should have appeared as a ghost, scaring the living daylights out of her. Would have served her right. She laughed at the thought.

Anna and her stepson, Jan, had moved back in with Mutter after being bombed out. Anna was the bright one of the four siblings. A straight-A student, her dream had always been to become a biologist, much to the dismay of their very traditional parents. They had not permitted her to enroll at university – not until the day Anna had moved out and taken her fate into her own hands. At least to Anna, the war had been good. Without it her mentor, Professor Scherer, would never have considered a woman for the job in his research department.

Worry crept into Lotte's heart again. It had been more than a year since her brother Richard's last letter. Several weeks later, the military command in Poland had sent a telegram to Mutter saying that Richard was *missing in action.*

What a dreadful term. *Gone missing.* As if he was some inanimate object that wasn't placed in its usual location. Did they expect to find him one day? Perhaps when they took a day off to clean the barracks, they'd be surprised to find him among hidden toys under the bed or behind the closet? She giggled hysterically at the notion.

Richard was her favorite sibling. Only one year older than her, they had fought like cats and dogs through most of their childhood. But they had also loved each other with a fierceness she hadn't felt for her sisters, who were four and five years older than she. Deep in her heart she knew he was alive.

Somewhere.

She would have felt it if he had died.

Yes, she would.

CHAPTER 11

"It's so incredibly boooooring," Lotte complained. They'd arrived in Denmark a week ago and there was no indication they would ever leave this darned garrison and the makeshift barracks. "We can't even go into town, because there is no town."

"Just flatlands, wind and rain," Agatha, an auxiliary of the *Kriegsmarine*, chimed in. "And I thought my work in Stavanger was dull."

Right now every woman would have, in the blink of an eye, chosen the dullest work over sitting around in boredom.

"Let's make a run for home. Nobody will even notice whether we're gone or not," Lotte whispered when she was alone with Gerlinde.

"You're stir crazy, woman."

"I have studied the map, it's not that far. And we can probably catch a train somewhere," Lotte said.

"Not far? It's at least three hundred miles. This place is

messing with your mind. What would you tell the conductor?" Gerlinde disguised her voice and said, "Excuse me, sir, we're Wehrmacht deserters and would like to go home."

Lotte couldn't help but start giggling and elbowed her friend. "Of course not, I'd go about it more diplomatically."

"Ah, and since when is diplomacy one of your talents, young woman?"

"If we stay here, I'm gonna die of boredom real soon." Lotte sighed.

"Believe me, it's better to die of boredom than being shot as deserters." Gerlinde shook her head at the antics of her friend. "Hang on for a few more days, the war is all but over. Haven't you heard?"

"Heard what?" Lotte pricked up her ears. Rumors of imminent surrender had been running wild for days, but nothing definite reached them.

In the next few days, events happened thick and fast. In the late evening of the first of May, the garrison command announced that the Führer Adolf Hitler had committed suicide. The new chancellor was propaganda minister Goebbels and Commander-in-Chief of the Navy Großadmiral Karl Dönitz the new president of the Reich.

A murmur buzzed through the ranks and Lotte saw the expressions of shock on virtually every face. Relief, horror, betrayal, depending on the person, but always paired with shock. Even the most zealous Nazis couldn't believe in a German victory anymore.

Her own expression probably reflected shocked cheer,

for this was the end of an era she had hated with all her heart – so much, she'd become a traitor to her own nation.

She felt a collective swaying in the ranks, as if they'd been struck by a true tragedy. Almost like children who'd been orphaned and now looked at each other for a clue about how to continue with their lives.

"It's not the end," one of the soldiers murmured.

"It is," someone else replied.

The next day the news of another suicide reached them: new chancellor Joseph Goebbels had preferred to follow the example of his Führer and evade accountability for the crimes he'd committed.

But what shocked Lotte to her core was that he and his wife Magda had first killed their six children before taking their own lives. She dropped to the ground, unable to fathom such cruelty.

"How could they? ... their own children," she stammered helplessly.

"Such a vicious thing to do," Gerlinde said, taking Lotte's hand.

"Better than having to live under the enemy," someone murmured.

Lotte stared at the offender and scolded him, "How pathetic you are! How can you approve of a man killing his innocent offspring just because he's too cowardly to face the consequences of his doings?"

"Cowardly? Goebbels was a fantastic leader!"

Lotte pummeled into the soldier's stomach to give him a well deserved trouncing. Not that she had any illusion about who would win a fistfight, but so pent-up were her tensions she longed for some physical violence to get rid of them.

If it hadn't been for Oberführerin Littmann's swift intervention, she'd be bloody and broken in some hospital by now. Instead, she was confined to the barracks building for an indefinite time.

But the flow of news didn't stop, just because she'd lost her equanimity. The city of Hamburg capitulated; British-American troops reached Lübeck and Wismar, effectively cutting off the northernmost part of Germany bordering with Denmark from the rest of the Reich.

The commanders-in-chief of Holland, Denmark and Norway were called upon to meet with Großadmiral Dönitz in Flensburg. The same evening, the radio announced the partial capitulation of Northern Germany and the occupied regions in Scandinavia to the Western Allies.

"The war is over!" someone screamed outside and Lotte took this as the sign that together with the war, her confinement had also ended. She ventured outside to see men and women cheering and lying in each other's arms, but only for a few short minutes until disenchantment settled amongst them.

"We survived," Gerlinde voiced the common train of thought. "But what will happen to us now?"

"Prisoners of war," someone said.

Those three words crawled down Lotte's back making her neck hair stand on end. She'd never really given a thought to what would happen to her after the war. She'd somehow assumed she'd simply go home.

While technically the female auxiliaries weren't

Wehrmacht soldiers, they still were Wehrmacht employees in uniform and as such would be treated the same as their male counterparts. Or so they said... although she'd heard horror stories as well.

Wehrmachtshelferinnen had been sent to perform slave labor in Russian Gulags, or worse, to brothels to "entertain" Red Army soldiers. Her entire being froze over even thinking about such a fate.

"Perhaps they'll send us home?" Agatha said.

"Home? I don't even have a home!" Gerlinde pushed a loose strand of hair behind her ear. "Where will they send me? My hometown now belongs to Russia."

"I'm sorry." Lotte wrapped her arm around Gerlinde's shoulder. "If they send us home, you can come with me."

"Thank you." Gerlinde surreptitiously wiped a tear from her eyes.

But nothing happened. Not for days. Some parts of the Wehrmacht were still fighting, most notably in Berlin, and the first Allied soldier had yet to set foot into Denmark. So, they kept waiting.

A nervous tension settled over all of them, because General Lindemann had given orders not to surrender to the Danish Resistance, but only to the Allied troops. Both sides were sitting on a powder keg, waiting to explode, until the first British soldiers finally arrived one week later. To say they were surprised to find a bunch of females in uniform would be an understatement.

"From the frying pan into the fire," said Agatha, who fought off sexual advances daily, like most of the other young women in the camp. Deprived of proper job descriptions and male line superiors who would penalize would-be suitors that stepped out of line, the Wehrmachtshelferinnen had lost their standing.

Despite Oberführerin Littmann's best efforts, the soldiers in the garrison regarded it as their inherent right to conquer the women, and their insistent efforts became more annoying and even frightening by the day.

"We shouldn't believe all the propaganda that is spread," Gerlinde said. "Can't be worse than what we have to bear now."

"I'd be happy to see the back of this sorry place with its ghastly weather. Can you believe that we're well into May and have yet to see a ray of sunshine?"

The next day, everyone in the garrison was put in open trucks and transported to a makeshift prison camp someplace inland. Men and women were separated along the way and the women were herded into the empty gymnasium of a school to be processed. A double row of coiled barbed wire surrounded the compound giving Lotte violent chills, as deeply stashed memories surfaced in her soul.

"Name?" a British soldier asked her.

"Alexandra Wagner."

"Rank?"

"Nachrichtenhelferin, radio operator."

"ID number?"

"589452," she said, still captured in her memories.

The soldier stared at her with wide eyes. "Excuse me?"

For a moment she didn't understand his concern and looked at him with a blank expression.

"That is not a valid number," he explained.

Slowly, it dawned on her. She'd given him her prisoner number from Ravensbrück. With a quick glance at him she decided it was best not to let anyone know about her real identity as Charlotte Klausen – not yet. With no proof whatsoever they wouldn't believe her anyway.

"Sorry." She reeled off her Wehrmacht ID number for him.

The conditions in the new quarters were even more deplorable than before. This was a school that had long been used for storage purposes. And the sanitary installations looked exactly like that: abandoned.

The water tubes must have frozen solid during winter and when Lotte opened the faucet only drops of brown slime appeared. She sniffed with disgust and decided that washing would have to wait.

Never one to dwell on bad circumstances she grabbed a solitary broom standing in a corner and began sweeping the floor. Soon, the other women joined her, using scarves and kerchiefs to wipe the worst of the dust and grime from windows, floors and walls.

After several hours of hard work, Lotte's back ached and she stretched out, handing her broom to Agatha. "Here, take over for a while, will you please?"

With a proud smile Lotte scrutinized the work they'd done so far. The place still didn't look inviting, but at least it was bearable. In the evening Oberführerin Littmann returned from her interrogation and gasped in surprise. "Well, *Mädels,* you have done a great job!"

She waved at her subalterns, raising her voice. "Gather around, girls, I have some news."

Lotte was dying to know what would happen to them and she joined the others standing in a tight circle around the older woman.

"Frankly, the British are overwhelmed with the number of prisoners they have captured and it will take a while until they manage to process everyone. Apparently last week the supreme command gave the order to discharge all female auxiliaries, but due to the capitulation this order never reached us here. The British have promised to proceed and discharge as fast as they can. But they have to address more pressing issues first.

"For one, they need to organize transport back to Germany and they will have to set up collection camps for those who don't have a home to return to." Littmann's gaze wandered over to Gerlinde and a few of the other girls from areas that now belonged to Russia, Poland or Czechoslovakia.

"Frau Oberführerin, how long will this take?" someone asked.

A tired expression etched itself into Littmann's face. "I cannot say. A few days, maybe a week, or two. All we can do is stay put and cooperate as much as possible."

The women started whispering, and the Oberführerin didn't stop them. It seemed she herself was too downhearted to keep up discipline.

What Lotte hated most about their new quarters were the toilets. Since there was no running water, they had to go outside to relieve themselves in a makeshift latrine – always at risk of running into one of the guards, who embarrassed the women with their prying eyes and obscene talk. She soon learned to never go alone and always have another woman stand watch to block the men from *accidentally* catching a glimpse.

Every morning a delegation of women was sent to

collect water from a nearby river. Under the scrutiny of their guards, who never moved a finger to help, they filled rusty steel barrels with water and lugged the heavy containers to their quarters.

The prisoners had long since forgotten the luxury of a bath, but Lotte delighted in doing a cat's lick once a day, washing her face, hands and neck. Since there was no privacy, she never dared to open her blouse or push up her skirt to wash the bare skin beneath.

After one such trip Lotte decided to come out. She didn't have illusions that they'd treat her like royalty if she told them her secret. But maybe she didn't have to suffer those deplorable conditions anymore.

So, she went to talk to the base commander.

"What do you want?" he asked her in a rather harsh tone.

"Sir, I wanted to inform you about my work for the Norwegian resistance."

"We're in Denmark." He looked at the papers in front of her.

Cleary, he wasn't interested in her story, but she tried again. "I know, but the British SOE—"

"Tell this to someone else. I have work to do," he said, dismissing her.

With sunken shoulders Lotte returned to her friends. It had been worth a try.

Food was scarce and irregular. As the Oberführerin had warned them, the Allies had more pressing issues to attend to than feeding their prisoners. In some way Lotte could understand. Everyone had been suffering from the rationing and just because the war was over didn't mean that food supplies miraculously multiplied and shortages disappeared.

Without the well-oiled machine of requisitioning and commandeering the best things for the German occupiers, they now switched places with the Danish population, who claimed most of the food for themselves, leaving only scraps for the hated oppressors.

Actual food lacking, the women resorted to talking about it – all the time.

"To celebrate the end of the harvest, my father would have a pig slaughtered," Gerlinde dreamed. "The *Erntedankfest* was a gluttonous good time of fine wines and delicious food. My granny used to make the finest bloodwurst and liverwurst far and wide."

Lotte's mouth watered at the vivid descriptions and she could actually smell the vinegary scent of sauerkraut that usually accompanied these traditional sausages.

"And the beer, don't forget the beer," a woman from Munich said, licking her lips and making a gesture of wiping foam from her mouth. "The golden liquid with the bitter taste."

"I remember how we had to spend our summer vacation picking hops in the Holledau region. It was some damned exhausting work," a blonde, thin girl said.

"You were there too? When?"

A conversation ensued about the advantages of picking hops versus collecting potato bugs or any other of the *voluntary* agricultural work schoolchildren had been forced to do.

Lotte's mind drifted back to her Aunt Lydia's farm, where she'd spent many summers with her family, helping with the harvest, playing with her brother Richard and her many cousins. Once the war started her mother had sent her to live with Aunt Lydia for almost two years to keep her away from Berlin and out of trouble.

That had worked only until Rachel, a Jewish neighbor about the same age as Lotte, had shown up in the barn with her three younger siblings. Lotte willed the memories away. They were too sad.

"Hey, Alex, what are you thinking about?" Gerlinde elbowed her.

"What? Me?"

"Yes, you. You had an expression on your face as if you'd stepped into purgatory."

She shrugged, fighting back her tears. Having to think about the death and suffering she had caused with her impulsive actions would be her personal hell for the rest of her life. Ever since, everything she'd done had been an attempt to make up for her well-meant but ill-conceived acts that had caused her friends to die.

Dark clouds invaded her soul as the dank reality sank in. As much as Lotte had yearned for the war to end, she now became aware that things would only get worse – for her and so many others. In Norway they'd been in a very comfortable position, far away from the theaters of war where the real action happened.

"Oh, goodness, Gerlinde," she suddenly whimpered. "Do you think there will even be a Berlin left to return to?"

"Why would you even want to go there? Didn't your family live in Cologne, before... you know... they died?"

Lotte choked on her slip-up. "Well, I know for sure there's not a stone left intact in Cologne so I thought the capital might be a good place for me to start my new life."

"Quite the adventurous type you are, Alex. What I wouldn't give to be able to return to my home."

CHAPTER 12

O ver the next days, more and more female auxiliaries from all over Scandinavia reached the holding camp, and in addition to food and hygiene, space became scarce.

Lotte almost wept with relief when finally it was announced they would be returned to Germany. No further details were given and wild imaginings abounded.

According to some secret key, they were divided onto military vehicles in groups of twelve. Most of the women from her unit ended up on different trucks, but by some divine miracle, at least Gerlinde stayed by her side.

"I'm so glad we're in this together," she confessed as they settled inside the smallish confines of the truck. It was cast in twilight, as the only light entered through holes in the canvas walls.

"We're going home. Isn't that exciting?"

"I'll believe I'm home when I see my family." For some

reason, Lotte had a bad feeling and she feared the worst for her family. The pictures she'd seen in the newspaper were devastating. There was nothing left to speak of in her beloved country. All major cities had been reduced to rubble by the incessant bombing and she hadn't even recognized Berlin from the aerial photograph on the front page.

How anyone could live amidst such utter devastation was beyond her imagination. She wished she could send a postcard to her mother, telling her she was coming home. But with the paper shortage and the postal service not working, this was wishful thinking.

"Where are we going?" someone asked as two British soldiers came to secure the flap to the tailgate.

"Shut up, bitch," one of them said, spitting on the floor and yanking the door closed.

The man's rudeness put a damper on Lotte's excitement at going home. She had seen the unabated hate in the eyes of the young man. Hate and grief. So many youths on both sides wouldn't make it home.

"What a nasty chap," a pretty redhead called Hertha complained.

"He has every right to be nasty, after what we did."

"We did? I did nothing wrong," another woman complained.

Lotte bit her tongue. It was best to keep silent and not stir the emotions already running high. The girl might actually believe what she said. So many had closed their eyes to the atrocities happening and had deluded themselves into believing thinly fabricated lies.

Labor camps for the work-shy. Re-education camps for troubled youth. Resettlement for the Jews. She'd bet her right arm that none of the women in the truck had ever been inside a concentration camp and suffered first hand from the inhumane treatment.

"Shush, I can hear the men argue," a big-boned brunette girl said.

"Whattaya understand, Maria?"

"Billund. They want to drop us off in Billund. Oh no, the sergeant says they have to take us to Gram. They complain it's too far and they have leave tonight…he canceled the leave…our drivers are furious."

Loud banging of the driver's cab doors as they slammed shut interrupted Maria's translation.

"Very furious, indeed." Lotte giggled, which earned her elbow punches from left and right.

"Not funny!"

The motor roared into action and the vehicle bolted forward.

"We're moving," Gerlinde said needlessly.

"Gram? From there it's not too far to the border at Flensburg," Hertha said.

"That's where my sweetheart was stationed. Do you think I'll find him there?" Maria asked.

"Dream on," Gerlinde laughed. "He'll be long gone, marched off to some prison camp."

"If he even survived…" Hertha said, and Maria made a face as if she might cry.

"Sorry, I didn't mean to disturb you. It's just… this bloody war…" Hertha grimaced. "I was quite happy with my life. Had just started my apprenticeship as seamstress when they conscripted me into this bloody uniform."

"You were conscripted?" Lotte asked, her eyes round. "I thought the female auxiliaries were strictly voluntary."

"Usually yes, but in some cases when there weren't enough women in a district joining up, the party leaders would just conscript girls to make their numbers," a woman in her late twenties explained.

"You have no idea the hoops I had to jump through to even be considered for joining up," Lotte said.

"Didn't your parents give permission?" Hertha asked.

"They… were long dead when I decided to join up. Bombed out in Cologne. I was lucky to get out with my life."

Everyone in the truck nodded. Each of them witnessed enough air raids to last for many lifetimes and lost more relatives and friends than they dared to keep track.

The journey took many hours, and they stopped every few minutes, waiting. Maria pressed into the corner peeked out a hole between the canvas and the solid side, relaying what she saw.

"The road's in real bad condition and I haven't seen so many vehicles in years. It's like evening traffic in Munich before the war."

"Oh, yes." Lotte remembered how it had been in Berlin, before gas rationing and the commandeering of private vehicles for military purposes.

"And soldiers… so many..." Maria said.

"What nationality?"

"Can't see… oh, wait. That's ours in *feldgrau*. Must be thousands being marched around. Over there, that must be British, I believe, by the happy smiles on their faces."

Lotte leaned back, closing her eyes as she listened to Maria's chatter. She could have done without it, but the others seemed intent on knowing what happened outside their little confines.

"Ah, a beautiful castle. It looks completely intact."

"Maybe that's where we'll be going," Hertha said and the others laughed. "There may even be a handsome prince there, waiting to welcome you, Maria."

"I doubt if a handsome Danish prince will look at you kindly, my girl," Gerlinde objected. "They kind of disliked it when we invaded their country."

"Ah, but Danish soldiers were disarmed without a fight and let go, and those captured were allowed to return to their units," Hertha laughed. "Don't you think that earns us some lenience?"

"No, I don't believe they share your sentiments, dear," Gerlinde wouldn't relent, but Lotte knew she purposely kept the witty banter going to keep up morale.

"Some of the lorries are going elsewhere." Maria made the observation from her peephole.

"Probably splitting us up for convenience."

"We're sticking together, Gerlinde." Lotte clutched her friend's arm tightly.

"There are quite a lot of people on the roads, traveling with their belongings. I wonder who they are and where they're going."

Lotte jumped as the truck plummeted into a pothole. She shrieked when her bum hit the hard floor again and searched for something to hold onto. Gerlinde came to her rescue and pushed her upright again.

"Oh my, that hurt." She rubbed her behind, hoping this journey would end soon. The truck came to a screeching halt and she bumped her head against the canvas wall. *Bloody driver.* The door of the driver's cab opened and slammed shut.

"Seems we've arrived at our destination," Lotte said.

After a while, the motor started up, the vehicle set into motion and then stopped again. The flap opened and the two soldiers driving them appeared. One of them pointed his rifle at the women, while the other one said, "Get down, everyone."

One woman after another jumped down from the truck bed, walking unsteadily on stiff legs. Lotte gave her surroundings a once-over and from what she saw, they were inside a former German garrison that now hosted British forces.

Huge numbers of soldiers milled about, but as far as she could see her group of women were the only German prisoners, and the only females. The fine hair on her neck rose up and she wondered why their guards had brought them here. They were frog-marched to a dilapidated hut at the very end of the compound.

"We're just grabbing a bite before bringing you to the prison camp," the younger of the two soldiers explained. "You wait here."

Then the two men disappeared and locked the door behind them. Lotte inspected her new prison. The hut must have previously been used as stables, for there were two horse boxes with earthen ground, leftover straw, a tiny storage room and a sink. She walked over to open the faucet and much to her surprise, it actually worked and fresh, clear water came rushing out.

Greedily she formed a bowl with her hands and drank her fill, then washed her face and hands in a cat's lick before her impatient comrades shoved her from the delightful source of liquid to refresh themselves.

"What do you think they'll do with us?" Gerlinde sidled up alongside her, pacing the small hut to get the blood in her legs flowing again.

"You heard them. A POW camp around here."

"But why did we stop here first? It doesn't make sense."

Lotte scoffed. "Nothing makes sense since we left Stavanger in a rush. That private was too hungry to carry on."

Hertha joined their conversation. "I'll bet I'm hungrier. We haven't had a bite since morning."

"Don't even mention food."

"It won't take long. I'm sure we'll get something once they've processed us in the camp."

"What makes you so sure?" Gerlinde pursed her lips. "So far the victors haven't shown a great deal of organization."

Lotte was willing to cut the Allies some slack. "You have to give them credit. Feeding enemy prisoners is probably not a high priority on their list."

"I just want to return to my family," Ada, a very young-looking girl, said.

"How come you're even here? You're how old?" It was the more mature Hertha who asked the question.

Ada paled. "My parents wouldn't allow me to join up, so I fibbed a tiny bit with my age. But I turned eighteen last month."

"How stupid of you!" Gerlinde threw up her hands and Ada looked as if she wanted to cry.

A wave of empathy engulfed Lotte. She'd been impulsive and stubborn like Ada when she was her age. Even though she had only two years on her, it felt like a decade. Or two. So much had happened.

I have changed.

CHAPTER 13

After what seemed an eternity, Lotte heard the boisterous, loud voices of drunken men.

"Probably still celebrating their victory," Gerlinde said. All over Europe spontaneous celebrations had broken out in the days after the capitulation.

Although the Germans didn't have a reason to celebrate, except showing secret relief that the dragged-out war was finally over, they'd witnessed many such occasions during their captivity.

"I hope our drivers won't be too wasted and forget about us," Lotte said. As strange as it sounded, she longed to arrive at the POW camp, hoping they'd be given food, a blanket, and a place to lie down.

Moments later the hut door was unlocked and a soldier, unsteadily swaying on his feet looked inside. He took out his package, getting ready to pee. Only then did he notice the gasping Ada and scratched his head. He turned around and peed outside the hut, mumbling something unintelligible to his comrades.

"What was that?" one of the women whispered.

"A drunken soldier," Hertha replied.

"Is he gone?"

Three more men poked their heads inside.

"I'm afraid not," Lotte said, fear creeping into her bones.

"What are you pretties doing here?" one of them said, and after recognizing their uniforms, he repeated the question in heavily accented German.

"Waiting to be taken to the camp," Hertha answered.

"Eh…" He seemed to think for a few moments. "Why don't we shorten your waiting time?"

"That would be nice," Ada said with a smile on her face. Lotte had a bad feeling about the situation, although she couldn't say exactly why.

"One moment. Be right back." His face lit up with a leering smile and he staggered outside, calling for his comrades, "Come here, there's a bunch of warm and nice girls waiting for us!"

Hoping she had misheard the words, Lotte felt the blood draining from her face. Surely, her English was too bad and she'd misunderstood. Surely…

About ten soldiers in different states of drunkenness stumbled inside and the one who'd first talked with the women stepped toward Ada.

"Come here, my lovely," he said, crooking her finger at her.

She dutifully obeyed, a shy smile on her face, and the next moment Lotte wanted to scream. The soldier swiftly squeezed her against his body, pressing a sloppy kiss on the young girl's mouth.

Ada was too stupefied to put up any kind of resistance, but Maria, who stood nearest to her, had fast reflexes and punched him in the shoulder.

"Ouch!" He let go of Ada and turned around to look at Maria, apparently unsure about what was going on. "What's wrong?"

"What's wrong? She's not even eighteen and you're falling over her like a wild animal." Maria glared daggers at the foreign solder.

"That's because he is," one of his compatriots said. "Johnny's a real tiger in the sack."

"Ughh… you're drunk. Leave us alone," Maria demanded.

"Nah… That peachy little blonde wanted me to shorten her waiting time, so just because you're jealous…"

"There's enough of us to do all of you, no need to be jealous," another man said.

Lotte swallowed hard. She had enough experience with Wehrmacht soldiers to know there was no way to rationalize with a drunken group of men. For this very reason, the girls always stayed in groups and the men's superiors usually kept a tight regimen. But right now, she couldn't hope for the help of an officer, as there seemed to be none around.

And who would come to the rescue of a bunch of enemy POWs anyways? She pressed against the wall, attempting to make herself invisible as she watched the horrible show unfolding.

"Come on, sweetie. It won't be to your disadvantage," Johnny said. "We'll bring you chocolate."

Meanwhile Ada had wised up to the men's plans and was hiding behind Maria's back, which didn't faze Johnny in the slightest. He mumbled something and then shrugged, grabbing the next best woman standing around, Hertha.

His mates cheered him on. "A kiss. Give her a kiss!"

Hertha struggled against the strong man who pressed a kiss on her lips. When he came up for breath, she slapped him and yelled, "Get your hands off me! Tommy bastard!"

Oh, no. Lotte could see a switch flip in his face as he stepped back growling at her, "What'd you call me, Nazi bitch?"

"Tommy bastard. And… coward," Hertha repeated, emphasizing her words with a kick to his shins.

"Ouch," he yelled and a hard expression entered his eyes. "I'll show you who's the boss around here. We fought your kind for years all through Europe; you think we can't handle a bunch of Nazi whores?"

Then he thrashed her to the ground and followed suit, ripping open her blouse. Hertha screamed at the top of her lungs, but not for long. Some helpful comrade of his quieted her with his big hand over her mouth.

"Leave her alone, you filthy beast!" Maria sprang forward, only to be captured by another of the Tommies.

"No need to be impatient, love, there's enough for all of you." His bloodshot eyes fixated on her skirt and he pushed it up, feeling her up.

Lotte thought she'd faint. Such horrible things she'd had to listen to but never watch. Not even in Ravensbrück when the vile Doktor Tretter had… her entire body froze over, making it impossible to react when one of the soldiers came over and began groping her under her clothes.

"You'll like it, ducky." His slurred words were meant to assure her.

She wanted to punch him, scream, kick, or do anything at all to fight. But the fact was, she couldn't even close her eyes during the assault, because deep-seated shame disabled the slightest movement of her body. The only part of her that still functioned was her heart, pumping frozen blood into her limbs, each thump more violent than the one before.

When the thumping stopped with a groan, a heart-wrenching whimper startled her out of her deathly rigidity. And together with the melting of the frozen cells in her body, her sorrows dissolved, leaving her disorientated.

Her wide opened eyes softly closed and pure, sweet darkness engulfed her. It became quiet and she floated high in the air, looking down at the sorry bunch of violated women and the drunken jollity of the retreating soldiers who'd sated their greedy appetites.

Those she'd helped to rid the world of the Nazi evil had been the ones to inflict this cruel treatment on her. Hadn't she believed the British were better than her own? A nation with morals and high ethical standards? She crouched in the corner, her body aching and her soul weeping.

The revelation came as a shock.

Good and evil didn't belong to nations, races, religions, or even ideologies. A man could fight for the right cause and for freedom, but still think he had the right to take from a woman what he wanted.

She balled her hands into fists, swearing to God that

she'd never let this happen to her again. She vowed that she would never forget, would never allow herself to be so vulnerable again.

It was in this dark moment that her youthful impulsive stubbornness returned and she made a promise to herself. Once she returned home she'd become a lawyer and fight for justice. She'd fight for all those who wouldn't be heard otherwise and would bring justice back into the world.

Yes, she would.

CHAPTER 14

Gerlinde lay unmoving a few feet from her. She crawled toward her friend and tried to shake her awake. Gerlinde stirred and looked at Lotte through tormented eyes.

"Are you alright?" Lotte asked, although she knew the answer already. How could any woman be alright after what had just happened?

"I guess so…" Gerlinde's feeble voice trembled.

"We need to get out of here."

"What?" Gerlinde opened her eyes wide.

Lotte dropped her voice to a low whisper, "In their stupor they left the door unlocked. That's our chance to escape."

"That's illegal. We're prisoners of war."

"So what?" Lotte put an unruly strand of her fiery red hair behind her ear. "What those men did was illegal, so we have every right to escape."

"Alex, please…"

"I for one am not going to sit around and wait for this to happen again. So, are you coming with me or not?" Lotte could see the internal war raging in her friend and she added, "Please?"

"I'm not sure... even with the door unlocked, won't there be guards around the compound? We're inside a garrison after all."

Lotte cocked her head, mulling over Gerlinde's words. Then she shrugged. "Know what? You rest and I'll check the situation. When it's clear I'll come and get you."

Her friend gave a weak nod and slumped to the earthen ground. None of the other women stirred, they'd succumbed to a deathlike sleep, their minds busy blocking out the horrible ordeal.

Her eyes fell on a forlorn dusty kitbag hanging on the wall, no doubt belonging to the new owners of the garrison. She snatched it from the hook and slung it across her shoulders before she got up and slid through the door, leaving it ajar.

She wondered why the slightest blue stripe dotted the horizon. Then she remembered. The endless summer nights this far north. Nearing the end of May, it would soon stay light throughout the entire night. The extra illumination wasn't exactly conducive to her purpose of sniffing out a way to escape, but on the other hand, it would be more difficult to find her way in absolute darkness. She'd just have to be more careful not to be seen.

The compound greeted her with absolute silence, all the soldiers seemingly fast asleep. She stayed in the shadows of the huts until she came to a huge building that she recognized as the mess.

Where there's a mess, there must be a kitchen. She slid inside through the unlocked door and waited until her eyes had adapted to the near-bleakness inside the room. Thinking that all garrisons looked more or less the same she went to the back wall, and sure enough, a door led into the kitchen.

She didn't dare to switch on the light, and fumbled around following the mouth watering-aroma of smoked ham until she found what she was looking for: the food storage. Rummaging in the storage, her hands touched a soft, light-colored block and she brought it to her nose. The smell of ripe cheese was so maddening to her starving stomach that she couldn't resist biting out a big chunk of it.

Hmmmm. She savored every last morsel, licking her lips, before she stuffed the rest of the block into the kitbag. A chunk of ham, a bread loaf and several tins that she hoped were army rations followed the cheese into her kitbag.

Then she felt through the drawers, until she found two things: a canteen and a huge butcher's knife. In the absence of other weapons, the knife would help them against would-be attackers.

As she filled the canteen with water from a tap, the temptation to keep the water running and give herself a good washing nearly overwhelmed her, but she was too afraid the noise would wake someone. *Nothing worse than being caught in a military kitchen stealing food.* So, she resisted the cool clean liquid and slipped out of the building.

The blue stripe on the horizon had disappeared, only starlight casting a peaceful light on the premises. For a moment she doubted her impulsive decision to escape. Except for the *incident* with the drunken men earlier, the new rulers had behaved appropriately.

99

According to Article 3 of the Geneva Convention, prisoners of war were entitled to respect for their persons and honor. Since the British soldiers had clearly violated her honor, she could report them. But after another moment of consideration she didn't give that endeavor much chance for success. Violations had happened even inside the Wehrmacht and never once had the man involved received more than a dressing-down, while the woman usually was shamed and released from service. *As if she had asked for it.*

Perhaps the best course of action would be to forget all about this, bury the *incident* deep down in her soul, along with so many other painful memories, and hope for the best. Since the Tommies weren't known to use rape on purpose, as a means to take revenge on the civilian population like the Ivan did, she might never find herself subjected to a similar situation again.

She should just chalk it up to a slip from proper behavior, caused by too much alcohol. An unfortunate *incident* that had caused no real physical harm, apart from a few scratches. But even as she tried to talk herself out of fleeing, her entire body convulsed into one tight knot.

Her despicable attacker might not have done her lasting bodily harm, but he had robbed her of something much more valuable. Her honor. Her dignity. The very core of her humanity. She gritted her teeth at the onslaught of excruciating emotions, doubling over and struggling to inhale.

The Nazis had tried to strip her of her humanity, not once but twice, and hadn't succeeded. She wouldn't let some fucking Tommy soldier achieve what the SS and Gestapo hadn't been able to do. She would not sit by idly and wait to become a victim again.

With her newfound determination she walked over to the hut where the other women huddled. Watching her comrades caught in sobbing nightmares, she nudged Gerlinde until her friend finally opened her eyes from a traumatic sleep.

Before she could scream, Lotte put her hand over Gerlinde's open mouth and said, "It's me. Alex. It's time to go."

A woman stirred and looked at them. "Where are you going?" she asked, half asleep.

"Pee," Lotte whispered back. "Do you need to go too?"

"No," the woman replied and closed her eyes again.

Lotte counted until twenty and then grabbed Gerlinde's wrist and pulled her out of the hut.

"The main entrance is lit up and guarded," she whispered at her friend. "But we can climb across the wall in the back."

Gerlinde did not utter a word. She followed Lotte like a puppet on a string to a place near the wall around the compound where a dog kennel stood.

"I'm not going anywhere near the dogs," Gerlinde said in a frightened whisper.

"No need to worry. I checked earlier. It's empty. Now come." Lotte had to bite back a giggle at the disgusted face of her friend. She couldn't fathom how a country girl could be so afraid of dogs. Lotte herself had never owned one, but she found them cute and friendly.

Lotte gave Gerlinde a leg-up onto the roof of the kennel and then Gerlinde extended her hand to help Lotte up. Up there she eyed the wall. It wasn't that big and she managed to put her hands on top.

"Ouch," Lotte hissed as a sharp pain stung her hand.

"Careful, there's glass shards." She handed the kitbag to her friend and struggled to heave herself up. Just when she was about to fling her leg over, the uniform skirt prevented the maneuver. She had to let go, because her hands wouldn't support her body weight much longer.

Damn skirt. It might look graceful but was damned impractical. Not only didn't it protect much against the damp chills in winter, but it also hindered free movement. *I should have been born a boy. I swear, I should.* A boy didn't have to wear skirts at all times. Could climb all the walls or trees he wanted. Wasn't a less worthy person in a world of men. And he certainly didn't have to endure what had happened earlier this evening.

Since there was no way to change that mishap of her birth, she pushed up her skirt all the way to her hips, exposing her torn undergarment.

"Alex!" Gerlinde's eyes clouded over with embarrassment as she saw the white material flashing against the dark night.

"There's no one to see us, so hurry up." *And what's there to see anyway since they already took what they wanted?* Lotte heaved herself up again, carefully feeling for the glass shards, and then swung her leg freely across the wall. Sitting astride, she took the kitbag from Gerlinde's hand and let it drop on the other side. Then she helped her friend up and they jumped down into the grass next to the kitbag.

Freedom! Lotte wanted to shout from the top of her lungs.

"Wow, that was all too easy," Gerlinde said, when they had put enough distance between themselves and the garrison and dared to speak again. "I think God is watching over us."

"Too bad He wasn't watching over us when those bastards forced themselves on us," Lotte retorted angrily. Regret plagued her the moment she spoke. What happened wasn't her friend's fault. "We must find a place to hide before the sun rises," she said in a conciliatory tone.

"Can't we walk by day?"

"Not really. We're still wearing our Wehrmacht uniform, and how long do you think it'd be until we'd be captured again?"

Even in the darkness Lotte could see the whiteness of her friend's face becoming more pronounced. She took her hand, assuring her, "That won't happen, though, as we'll be careful. Resting during the day and traveling by night." Right now her decision to escape didn't seem like such a bright idea anymore. But it was too late... returning inside was only possible through the main gate.

She gave a hysterical giggle as she imagined the situation. *Hello, guard. We took a stroll around the compound; would you be so kind to let us back in and lock us up?*

Gerlinde, though, seemed to wake up from her apathy and turned at Lotte. "We have to turn ourselves in. This is a suicide mission."

"I'm not." Lotte's entire body heated up with ire and an ache like no other shot through her core, reminding her of the violation. "I'm not going back. I prefer to be shot for escaping than..."

Gerlinde's face lost its striking paleness and Lotte felt the heat emanating from her friend's cheeks. "I'll turn myself in."

"Please don't." Lotte begged, "I can't do this on my own. Please. We won't get caught; I promise."

"How can you even promise such a thing?"

"Because… I won't ever allow a man to have his pleasure at our expense again." Lotte took out the butcher's knife from the kitbag. "Next time, I'm prepared."

"Good gracious, Alexandra. Put that thing away."

"Only if you come with me. Please, will you? Together we are invincible." Lotte begged and pleaded until her friend finally relented.

"Alright." Gerlinde hugged her. "Do we even know where we're going?"

"Not exactly. But I figured Denmark is such a small country and from Gram it's just walking south until we reach the border."

Gerlinde giggled, as they continued walking down the only road. "Says the woman who mastered Morse code as if it were her native language but is still lost when she has to locate a place on the map."

"See why I need you?" Lotte squeezed the hand of her friend.

"I'm starving," Gerlinde complained after a while.

"Oh, with all the excitement I totally forgot." Lotte reached into the kitbag and produced a chunk of bread.

"Oh, my sweet Lord! Where did you get this?" Gerlinde shoved the bread into her mouth.

"From the kitchen at the base," Lotte answered.

"You stole this from the kitchen?"

"Yes, I stole from the kitchen!" Lotte was furious. "Consider it payment for what those bastards stole from me. I'd say it's just fair, don't you think?"

"I'm sorry. I'm as hurt as you are, but rash and vengeful action won't help us."

"You're right." Lotte fell into silence, mulling over Gerlinde's words. She'd sworn never to act rash and irresponsible again. That she'd never again endanger her friends with her impulsiveness. Was history about to repeat itself?

CHAPTER 15

They walked along the deserted road under a dark sky full of stars until they came upon a crossing.

"Which way to take?" Lotte asked, moving her head from left to right.

"I wouldn't know, not until we can see the sun rising." Gerlinde flopped down on a rock by the side of the street. Her stomach gave a peculiar sound much like a wolf howling to the moon.

"I guess we could take a break and eat." Lotte carefully peered in all directions and especially from where they'd come. But the night was silent. Their absence wouldn't be noticed until morning. Then they'd be marked as absconders, fugitive prisoners of war. She hoped the British wouldn't put too much effort into searching for two missing women. The way they had treated them before, considering them a burden keeping the soldiers in charge from doing more important work, gave her the confidence to sit beside Gerlinde and open the kitbag.

She took out the butcher's knife and cut off generous slices of cheese, ham and bread for the two of them. Chewing on the food, she pondered their choices. Due to the time of year, the dawn would arrive in no time at all and they might as well rest here before they decided which road to walk. On the other hand, every minute they kept waiting heightened the risk of being found.

"We need to get the hell out of Gram," Lotte replied. "When they find out we're missing, I want to be as far away from this place as possible."

"It won't matter where we are," Gerlinde said, looking down her dirty Wehrmacht uniform. "In this attire, how long do you think it will take until someone notices we're escaped prisoners of war on the run and turns us in?"

"That's why we can't risk anyone seeing us. I sure don't want to get arrested."

"Please," Gerlinde chewed on her piece of ham. "Let's turn ourselves in. It might not be so bad."

"Yes, sure, you'll be forgiven if you turn yourself in," Lotte said sarcastically. "Hearts of gold, the British have. Have you enjoyed the little taste of their compassion last night?"

Gerlinde held her hands over her face and shook her head as if to erase the memory of the horrific assault. "Don't be cruel."

"It wasn't me who was cruel. But you seem to have taken complete leave of your senses. What exactly do you think they'd do with us?"

"The firing squad?" Gerlinde whispered. "I don't want to die now that the war is over. Have we made it through years of battle, even survived that bloodletting in Warsaw, just to be killed for desertion now?"

The desperation in her friend's voice swept away the bitterness Lotte felt and she touched Gerlinde's cheek. "I'm sorry. It's just... I'm so angry. It's like my blood is boiling with the thirst for revenge. I want to tear the entire world to pieces and hurt them a million times more than they hurt me." She stopped talking, knowing full well that this mindset would only serve to get her into more trouble. Two calming breaths later she said, "I'm sorry, Gerlinde. I won't take out my anger on you. You are my friend... it might have been better to stay in captivity, but we'll never know. Because, now, we cannot return."

"I know."

They finished eating and waited in silence until the pale light of a dawning sun appeared on the horizon.

"Look," Lotte said with excitement. "There's east."

"Then we take this road. It'll lead us south." Gerlinde smiled, the relief apparent. "From Gram to Flensburg, it's less than sixty miles."

"How do you know?" Lotte asked in wonder.

"It's all in here." Gerlinde tapped at her head. "Or what do you think I was doing while getting bored to death back home? I'd spend entire days poring over my atlas and imagining the places I could go."

"Good for us. Now let's walk."

They didn't have much time, because before morning broke and people left their houses they'd have to hide.

"I wish we'd taken our civvies."

"Me, too, but our suitcases were in that truck." Gerlinde

stopped and turned to look at her friend. The agony in her beautiful eyes split Lotte's heart in half.

"What's wrong?"

"The photograph of my family. It's in my suitcase. What if I never see them again and have now lost the only keepsake that keeps their memory alive?"

Lotte squeezed her hand. "You will see them again. I'm sure of that. Didn't they flee East Prussia in time before the Red Army arrived?"

"They did, but I haven't heard from them since. And the journey was dangerous…"

Words were inadequate comfort for Gerlinde's pain, so Lotte only could hold on to her hand and hope for the best. Until she remembered that her own photographs of her family had stayed behind, too. Tears pooled in her eyes and she blinked them away. Crying now would be akin to admitting they were dead. *I'll have plenty of opportunity to make new photographs together with them once I get to Berlin.* Instinctively, she felt for the one picture she kept with her at all times in the breast pocket of her blouse. Johann. Her fingers caressing the rigid paper, she suddenly had a clear image of him, carrying heavy logs to a lumber mill, feeding the gluttonous sawing machines.

His hands were raw and chapped, bleeding from the rough wood. His honey-colored eyes had lost their warm glow and taken on the empty look of desperation she knew so well from her time in Ravensbrück. It hit her square in the stomach and she doubled over, panting and spluttering.

"What's wrong?" It was Gerlinde's turn to speak these words, but Lotte only shook her head. Because… how could she explain a vision?

Hours later, before the morning fully broke, they ventured away from the road and came upon an empty shack leaning haphazardly against the remains of a tree that had been split in half.

"This is the perfect place to hide out and rest," Lotte said. Long since deserted, the shack was well off the beaten track and provided a perfect sanctuary for the fugitives.

"I guess it'll do." Gerlinde was considerably less enthusiastic.

The lush green openness provided a feast for Lotte's tired senses. The grass smelled fresh and tangy, the singing birds illuminated the mind and quieted the sorrows. "It's such a lovely place," she said, her face dreamy and her brain occupied absorbing all the beauty, stashing it deep inside her, ready to feed upon it again during the bleak night.

"Yes, it's lovely," Gerlinde agreed. "Nothing like it looked on our farm, but it still reminds me of the amazing wonders of nature."

"You must miss it so much."

"I do." Gerlinde did her best to keep a straight face, but Lotte wasn't fooled. Working day in, day out together, and sharing a room in the barracks hut, she knew her friend almost better than herself. She could tell with certainty the mood Gerlinde was in, knew her hidden fears, her deepest sorrows and her greatest joys.

In just a year's time she'd come to connect with Gerlinde in a way that had been reserved for her siblings – before they'd been torn apart, scattered to the four winds. Richard had been the first one to leave the family home in Berlin.

Conscripted into the Wehrmacht at the tender age of sixteen. Thrust into the Eastern Front with so many other boys, raw recruits with no life experience to account for, a leaf in the wind of fate. His chances of surviving this war had decreased with every passing day, and yet, hope remained.

So far, out of thirty classmates, twenty had returned home in the form of a laconic telegram stating, *Your son has given the ultimate sacrifice for Führer and Fatherland. There's no reason to grieve, only to be proud.*

Lotte involuntarily balled her hands into fists. Didn't the authorities know how much misery one of these dreaded telegrams caused? Did they have to mock the mothers, fathers, sisters, brothers, and girlfriends in such a spiteful way?

Even mourning wasn't allowed anymore. Shedding tears for a fallen soldier was akin to high treason. Out-of-their-mind mothers who blamed Hitler and his cronies for the death of their sons were dragged to the Gestapo headquarters to be taught a lesson about defeatism.

Her blood boiled with rage. Twenty dead. Five in Russian captivity. Two, one of them her brother Richard, missing in action. Three still fighting. That had been the situation two months ago when she'd last heard from her sister Anna.

Anna. Lotte sighed. She'd be forever indebted to her older sister for what Anna had sacrificed for her. A sacrifice that only now she could fully comprehend and that came nothing short of the *ultimate* one. Her heart tightened and the throbbing pain between her legs intensified. Anna had made it sound like it wasn't a big deal, nothing really to speak of. But Lotte had seen the unspeakable pain in her sister's beautiful blue eyes.

And Ursula, the oldest. The correct one. The good girl who never once was in trouble as a child, very much unlike tomboy Lotte, who never once was *not* in trouble. Ursula had surprised everyone, including Lotte, when she'd defied the Nazis in a way not many dared and had started working for a resistance cell, smuggling *undesirables* out of Germany.

"There's a creek." Gerlinde's voice pulled her out of her thoughts and she peered at her surroundings. The rolling greenery ended against a forested area and a clear stream meandered through tree-lined banks.

Lotte looked at the clear water and yelped, "Oh my goodness. I can't even remember the last time I properly bathed. I'm getting in."

Gerlinde giggled, but followed suit. The friends stripped down to their underwear and walked into the clear, chilly water. It was such a blessed feeling to be in the thigh-deep stream, the water softly tugging at her legs.

"Brrrr…" Lotte scrunched up her face into a grimace and inhaled deeply before she immersed herself completely. At first the chill took her breath away, but after a few seconds it was refreshing. She emerged from beneath the surface and beckoned, "Come in. It's heavenly."

"Heavenly cold." Gerlinde was bracing her arms around her shoulders, her lips quivering.

"Only for a moment. Come in and you'll see." Lotte dove in again and swam a few tentative strokes, before putting her feet down and glancing back at her friend. "Come on. What are you waiting for?"

Gerlinde theatrically pinched her nose and jumped into the deep waters. When she emerged moments later, a huge grin was spreading on her face. "You were right. It's swell to feel clean again. Too bad we don't have soap."

The girls began to wash out their hair with nothing but clear water, vigorously scrubbing sweat and grime from their heads, disentangling greasy strands, combing them with their fingers.

"You know," Gerlinde said with a pensive tone. "I never knew how much I would miss simple things like a hairbrush and soap. It's true that we don't appreciate what we have until we lose it."

Lotte stopped in her efforts to straighten the vicious knots in her fiery red curls. Since joining the Wehrmacht auxiliaries, she'd cut her magnificent over-shoulder-length hair to a more easily manageable chin-length modern bob. Still, her curls didn't take kindly to neglect and after days without a comb they were a tightly woven mess.

She glanced at her friend, whose honey-blond wet hair clung perfectly straight and without any visible entanglements, down to her shoulders. "Wow. I'm fighting an unwinnable battle against my knotted curls and you're talking advanced philosophy. What's wrong with me?"

Gerlinde giggled and splashed her with water. "Let me help you." With expert fingers she managed to transform the red mass of stubborn strands into something akin to a haircut and licked her lips with a satisfied smile when she said, "Ready. You look like an actual human being again."

"Thanks. Now I just need clean clothes to change into."

"We could wash…although…"

"…I'm not sure that's a good idea."

"We might attract less attention with dirty uniforms, should we be seen."

Lotte nodded. As usual, they seemed to know the other one's thoughts. They emerged from the water and lay on a grassy bank, letting their wet undergarments dry in the morning sun that blazed down on them.

"This is heaven," Lotte said dreamily.

"We still should get dressed and get some shuteye in that shack over there."

Lotte made a face but dutifully slipped into her dirty uniform and followed Gerlinde to the hut. It might have been the refuge of a forest warden in better times, or used by poachers during the war, but now it was an empty, dusted-over place full of cobwebs. An old mattress peeked out beneath dusty rubble and a three-legged chair perched against the wall.

They ate most of the provisions Lotte had taken from the British garrison, spiced up with forest strawberries and dandelion leaves Gerlinde had picked around the hut.

"We'll take turns sleeping," Lotte ordered, taking precautions even in a deserted area like this. Denmark was a small country and as such, nothing was far away from the next village. She didn't want to get caught unawares in her sleep.

CHAPTER 16

They slept through the day, taking turns standing guard, and started their walk toward the border again in the late evening. It was a slow process through the fields, because they could barely see a few yards ahead and stumbled along like drunken sailors.

"It's no use. If we continue at this pace, we won't reach the border before winter returns." Gerlinde said.

"It's June. Winter is at least four months away."

Gerlinde fell into a ditch she hadn't seen along the field and stretched out her hand for Lotte to help her out again. "See? We need to return to the road."

Lotte shook her head. "But then we can only walk under the cover of night and that will give us just a few hours each night."

"There are so many people on the roads, will it really matter if we walk during the day?" Gerlinde suggested. "I think it will be safer; besides, the extra hours will get us home faster."

"You have a point. But apart from looking the same as any other dirty, wretched individual, we're still in uniform."

"Oh, right. But... we need to cover more ground."

"Let's walk in the early morning and late evening. People still need to sleep during that time, even when it's not dark outside." Lotte scrunched up her nose, thinking.

"We really need to get civvies."

"And how exactly should we go about it? We can't very well walk into a shop and tell them we need to shed our uniforms."

"We could... organize them...?"

"Organize?" Lotte's jaw gaped open. "You gave me a dressing-down for stealing food from the garrison kitchen and now you suggest we go thieving clothes."

Gerlinde's face flushed red. "We could leave some money."

"What a grand idea! We'll leave a note with a couple of Reichsmark thanking the owner for their help."

"I thought..."

Lotte felt bad seeing the embarrassed expression on her friend's face and patted her arm. "It actually is a good idea, although I doubt the Danes will appreciate our Reichsmarks. I've heard the new favored currency is British pounds."

"...Or cigarettes. You don't have one, by chance?"

"No, my dear, not one." Smoking women were frowned upon in Nazi Germany and therefore the Blitzmädel didn't receive army provisions of cigarettes like the men did. Before today this had never posed a problem for Gerlinde, who only needed to flutter her eyelashes to get one.

"I could really use a fag." Gerlinde sighed, her eyes

becoming dreamy. "You should try it one day. It suppresses your appetite, makes you more alert and keeps the chill out of your bones."

"You should work for Reemtsma, praising the health benefits of their ciggies," Lotte giggled.

"Believe me, I would. Being a poster girl smiling down from an advertising column can't be all that bad."

Lotte all but toppled over in a fit of giggles. "Stop. Right now."

"Why?" Gerlinde joined her laughter and together they enjoyed a few minutes of uninhibited silly recklessness, before they sobered up to reality.

"We better continue walking; we still have a long way to the border."

And they walked trance-like along the road south, every step taking them closer to Germany.

One painful step after another.

Lotte had stopped talking, thinking, caring. She simply moved her feet, focused on ignoring the soreness between her legs that increased with every aching step she took.

At the end of the night, they ventured away from the road again, finding an uprooted tree that had left a cave-like hole in the earth. They cuddled, exhausted, sharing the warmth of each other's bodies. Forgotten was the need to take turns sleeping, to be cautious and stay alert; too dire was the fatigue. It engulfed them, slowed down their breathing and lulled them into deep slumber.

Not even the tickling rays of sunshine on her nose could wake Lotte from her dreamless sleep.

"Woof." A loud bark penetrated the air. "Woof. Woof." At the insistent repetition of the sound invading her sleep,

Lotte jerked up, her eyes wide open, staring into the sun high up in the sky, filtering through the leaves and blinding her for a moment.

She heard the ferocious growl and smelled the dog before she saw his furry face with sharp white teeth less than a yard away from her. Anguish attacked her heart, freezing her tightly in place, making it impossible to even blink an eye. Which was probably a good thing, because the vicious dog would have shredded her to pieces had she tried to run.

At the gulping sound next to her, Lotte turned her head the tiniest bit to see Gerlinde's frantic expression. Her friend looked as close to a heart attack as Lotte felt. The large dog barked again and she expected the animal to charge at them, sink his teeth into her tender flesh and rip it apart. Then, seemingly out of nowhere, an old woman strode toward the frightened girls. She had long, white hair, piercing green eyes, and skin leathered from decades exposed to the sun. She used a walking stick, but was surprisingly agile in her movements. The old woman looked exactly like the bad witch in Hansel and Gretel, and Lotte pursed her lips at the notion of being fattened up for a Sunday roast.

"Rex, sit!" The woman shouted her command at the animal, which obeyed her instantly. The walking stick turned out to be a rifle and its muzzle replaced the fangs of the dog in Lotte's range of vision. Crouched into the earth, Lotte knew the uniforms were giving them away.

"Get up, Nazis!" the woman ordered with a swift movement of her head. "But slow, or Rex here will take it out on you."

Gerlinde grabbed Lotte's arm, digging her fingernails deep into her flesh, clinging to Lotte as if she were a lifeboat. One glance at her friend's visage told Lotte that she had passed the state of fear and jumped right into mortal agony, making it impossible to obey the dog owner's commands.

"Need an extra invitation?" The woman pointed her rifle at the ridiculously shivering Gerlinde.

"No, ma'am. We're getting up now." Lotte wobbled to her feet, dragging Gerlinde up with her. They must have presented a picture of utter and complete misery. Two girls in Wehrmacht uniform, ragged, dirty, torn.

"Rex, heel," the woman ordered and a now docile German shepherd walked over to his mistress, eyeing the scene with interest. One word from the old lady and he would be back to challenge the trespassers.

"What are you doing on my property?" she demanded of the girls, looking ever more like the bad witch.

Lotte involuntarily squinted her eyes, searching for the gingerbread house. Catching her ludicrous behavior, she wondered about the strange ways a mind wandered when faced with death. For, the woman had no good reason not to shoot them.

Raising her hands in a gesture of surrender, she tottered unsteadily on her feet, Gerlinde half hiding behind her, shivering like aspen leaves at the sight of the German shepherd. Lotte's brain used the distraction to wander away from her imminent death and wondered what had caused Gerlinde's unnatural fear of dogs. She decided to ask her later, should they survive this ordeal.

As if Rex knew she was thinking about him, he growled a warning, baring his huge fangs, primed to attack.

"Please, ma'am, it's not how it looks," Lotte begged, noticing by the smirk on the old woman's face that her excuse was as lame as it sounded. "I m-mean y-yes, we are Wehrmacht auxiliaries, but we mean no harm."

"No harm! Your folks killed everyone I loved. I'll hand you over to the military police."

"I'm s-sorry. I really am. W-we escaped near death at the hands of the British and are now on the run. They'll shoot us for sure ..." Lotte had difficulties keeping her voice steady.

The woman scoffed. "I'd spare them the trouble and shoot you lot myself."

"Please," Lotte begged, her legs wobbly.

The woman suddenly frowned, her stare gliding down Lotte's leg. Now Lotte noticed it too, a slow trickle of warm liquid working its way down her leg. She gazed down to see the red trail and sighed, "Thank God."

"Thank God for what?"

"My monthly visitor." Lotte's cheeks flashed with embarrassment, despite the relief washing over her. She hadn't thought about the consequences the awful assault might have produced. How disgraceful it would have been to carry the proof of dishonor. Mutter had coped surprisingly well with the news that her oldest daughter Ursula was impregnated out of wedlock, but she would die of shame if her youngest one came home with the unwanted bastard of a nameless foreign soldier under her heart.

The woman's eyes filled with silent understanding. At her age she was well-versed in the weapons of war and the fates of beautiful young girls. Her expression softened and she looked over at Gerlinde, who was still a shivering mess, hiding behind Lotte's back. "What about your friend?"

"Her too," was all Lotte could utter. Pronouncing the awful word would be like reliving the assault again. She preferred to keep silent and never to think about what had happened.

"Should I take pity on these girls? What do you think, Rex?" the woman addressed her dog.

He perked up his ears, raising his snout in the air in a gesture resembling a nod.

"You think I should?" She furrowed her brows. "After all the Nazis have done to us? Look at their uniforms."

Rex dutifully turned his head and lazily got up, circling Lotte and Gerlinde. Lotte felt her trembling friend pressing tighter against her, her fingernails digging painfully into Lotte's arm. Neither one of them moved, frozen in place, while the dog finished his perusal, encouraged by his mistress.

"Why should I show them any pity?" she raged. "The Nazis murdered my husband in front of my eyes. They shot my son, left him to bleed out and die with his wife and daughter watching. Their kind does not deserve mercy. Doesn't the Bible say, 'An eye for an eye and a tooth for a tooth'?"

Rex trotted back to sit beside his mistress, apparently unsure how to respond. The old woman chucked his neck and Lotte seized the moment of compassion to make a case for herself and her friend.

"Ma'am, doesn't the Bible also say, 'Forgive us our trespasses, as we forgive those who trespass against us'?"

The woman's lips pursed. "Well-versed in the Bible. What's your name, girl?"

"Alexandra Wagner. Like you, I lost my family in this horrible war. A bombing over Cologne took everyone from me I loved." Lotte now had an idea how to spin her story. "I was petrified. Eaten up by hatred and a yearning for revenge. That's why I joined up as Wehrmacht auxiliary... that's the only reason why I'm wearing this uniform now. To avenge my family, my neighbors, my friends." She paused for a moment, fixing her stare on the old woman, willing her to soften up. "Look how it has served me, this need for revenge. Abused, assaulted and soon to be shot dead by another woman who has lost everyone she loves."

Behind Lotte's back, a strangled sob escaped from Gerlinde.

"Ah, it is a wicked world we live in when there is no difference between friend and foe. Enough killing has been done already." The old woman shrugged and lowered the barrel of her rifle.

Lotte pushed out the breath she'd been holding, but the vigilant eyes of Rex dared her to move.

"Follow me. I'm in the mood for bringing some good into this world of evil. The war's over. Come, Rex," the woman said gruffly and turned around.

Stupefied, Lotte didn't fall into step right away. Rex's low growl indicated he wasn't pleased with her lack of speed in following the orders of his mistress. She hurried to snatch the kitbag and matched the woman's pace, Gerlinde by her side, Rex bringing up the rear of the small procession.

After a good twenty minutes' march they came to a

clearing where a little cottage stood. It didn't resemble a gingerbread house, but a stab of fear still swept over Lotte. Yet there was no way to outrun a bullet, or a dog.

She had to trust the old woman, whether she wanted to or not. Gerlinde had recovered from her state of shock, now that the dog was out of sight trotting peacefully behind, and whispered, "She might look like a witch, but I don't believe we have any reason to fear."

Lotte hoped her friend was right.

CHAPTER 17

"The door is open; go on in!" The old woman nudged Lotte in the back with the barrel of her rifle. After a split-second of hesitation, she gripped Gerlinde's elbow tight and together they stepped through the heavy front door of the cottage. If the woman wanted to kill them, she surely wouldn't bring them into her home first.

"Better not be seen outside in those uniforms of yours," she said. "I'm Ingrid, by the way."

"Gerlinde Weiler."

"Gerlinde. Gentle javelin." Ingrid noticed the confusion and explained, "It's an Old High German name. *Ger* is a Germanic dart and *lind* means soft, gentle. The name was given to women of noble origins with a gentle character." She scrutinized Gerlinde for a long minute, before she continued, "The name is very fitting for you. Your gentle character may be hidden beneath your thirst to enjoy your life, but this is going to change with the years."

Ingrid turned toward Lotte, giving her a pensive look.

"Now, for Alexandra, that's an entirely different thing. It's derived from Alexander and the meaning is defender, protector. You have a strong sense of justice and seek to protect the weak, defend those treated unjustly. You'll go on to do great things with your life. The person who chose this name for you knows you very well. It's almost if she'd known you for years even before giving you the name."

Lotte staggered under Ingrid's unforgiving stare, which penetrated her very soul, ripping her entire being out into the open. That woman definitely was a witch, or why did she know things nobody else knew? Ursula had chosen the new name for Lotte and she'd known her for seventeen years...

Returning the stare, Lotte observed her vis-à-vis closely, realizing that in spite of the white hair and the leathery skin, Ingrid was not really an old woman. Only the deep furrows on her face, caused by sorrow, made her seem ancient. She might be the same age as Mutter, who was in her late forties.

Gerlinde broke the silence. "We don't want to impose on you."

"You are imposing," Ingrid said in a gruff tone. "But since I decided to end the blood for blood, as your friend suggested, I need to keep you away from prying eyes. What do you have in that kitbag of yours?"

"Just some bread, a knife and a water bottle," Lotte truthfully answered, although she omitted the money hidden in her shoe.

"No change of clothes?"

Both girls shook their heads in unison.

"I can't very well send you on your way in these

uniforms," Ingrid sighed. "Wait here!" Then she disappeared through one of the doors.

Lotte stood unsure, glancing over at her friend. But if she had entertained the idea of running away, an almost inaudible growl reminded her of Rex's presence. The German shepherd certainly wouldn't take kindly to their disobeying his mistress's commands.

So they waited.

Ingrid soon returned with two old, ragged dresses that resembled sacks. "Change into this."

In fashionable mouse gray, the coarse material just about scratched Lotte's skin by nothing more than looking at it. Death-defying, she took the dress into her hands, peering around for a place to change.

"It's only me and Rex, so no reason to be shy." Ingrid laughed. "Get behind that armchair if you must."

Lotte flushed bright red, the heat emanating from her ears. It wasn't so much that she was a prude who didn't dare to be seen in her undergarments by another woman, but more that she hated to reveal the bruises on her legs and arms, remnants of the proceedings she yearned to forget.

Taking imperfect cover behind the armchair she stepped out of her uniform and slipped into the dress that hung heavy from her shoulders with no form to speak of. Her suspicion that it really was a sack increased when she saw the faded black letters adorning the mousey cloth.

Once Gerlinde had changed into her new *dress*, Lotte almost had to giggle at the scarecrow coming out from behind the armchair. *At least no man will mistake us for beautiful prey in this attire.*

"Thank you, Ingrid. We appreciate your kindness,"

Gerlinde said, with the rigid posture of a queen even when adorned by the ugliest of sacks.

"I help you not out of the kindness of my heart, because I have none for you. I'm doing it to honor my Arne," Ingrid retorted with a shudder. "My Arne was an exceptional man. He fought those Nazi bastards to the very end, but he would never have laid one hand on a woman. He always told me to be compassionate even when it went against my being. Isn't it ironic that your people had no mercy for my Arne and yet it is he who has saved you now?"

Silence filled the cottage as each drifted off into her own private hell of painful memories, until a growl from Rex brought the women back to the present.

"You can stay here tonight. It's not safe to travel in the dark," Ingrid told them. "There are wild animals about and you could be attacked."

Lotte feared uniformed men more than wild animals, but she nodded in agreement with her hostess.

"But in the morning, you must leave. It is better that way."

"Yes, ma'am. We will be on our way in the morning," Gerlinde spoke up. "Thank you for your kind hospitality, we will never forget what you did."

"Enough of the sentimentality." Ingrid tried to put on a fierce front. "Better I get dinner ready."

"May we help you?" Gerlinde asked and Ingrid beckoned them into her small, homey kitchen. Sitting at the sturdy wooden table, the three women peeled and sliced and diced the ingredients for a hearty stew.

Tears sprung to Lotte's eyes and she said, "It's so long

since I did this with my mother and I never realized what a pleasure it was."

"Where is she now?" Ingrid asked, her face taking on a wistful expression.

"In Berlin." Gerlinde shot her a shocked stare. "She's dead, but my grandmother is in Berlin."

"I hear the Ivan has Berlin under his thumb, not wanting to give the other Allies their rightful share."

Stupefied, Lotte stared at her.

"Come on, you must have known this. Years ago, the Allies divided the booty amongst themselves, giving each a chunk of your country, and your capital. Germany as we know it has ceased to exist, never to rise from the ashes. It is annihilated, defeated, smashed into pieces. One for each of the four Allies," Ingrid scoffed.

"Although I don't know why France claims to be a victorious power, since they haven't fought any harder than others like Poland, Norway, the Netherlands or even Greece and Yugoslavia did. Except for our pathetic country of willing collaborators, every other nation in Europe fought against your bloody folks." Ingrid's words became more heated and she attacked the cabbage on the table as if she were flaying Nazis into tiny pieces.

"But I digress. Fact is, your country was cut down to the core, giving away pieces to the neighboring countries. And the tiny core area you have left is dismembered like the soldiers on the battlefields were. Divided into four parts, each one of them belonging to one of the victors, making sure your country will never again pose a threat to peace and the well-being of others. But because the Allies hate each other, they couldn't even agree on the booty. Each looking suspiciously to see if the other one has gotten the better chunk, much like siblings always fighting about toys, chores, and food."

Lotte's ears burnt with shame, but she had to know. "So what about Berlin?"

"Since it's the capital, everyone wanted to have it. It's the most coveted prize in this war. Set foot into Berlin and be forever the one who rules this world. So they decided to quarter the city as well. In spite of its location in the Soviet Zone, the Tommies, Amis and French get their part. How that will work out, I have no idea. Anyhow, the Ivan got there first and apparently has decided he'll keep Berlin for himself, not letting the other armies step inside. God, I sure hope those stupid men don't start another war over the fate of this condemned city." Ingrid looked up, gathering the vegetables into a pot.

"If you ask me, a malediction has been cast over Berlin. It will take many more decades and many more sacrifices until three wise men will come along. They will countermand the curse by overcoming their differences peacefully and joining their hands together. I won't be around by that time." Ingrid's green eyes gleamed like emeralds in the sun. "Your children and grandchildren will."

A lump formed in Lotte's throat at the ominous words. She couldn't imagine living the rest of her life under a constant doom. The old woman must have lost her mind grieving for her husband and son.

It turned out Ingrid was quite the enjoyable hostess who knew a lot more about politics, philosophy and earthly wisdom than one would expect from a simple woman living alone in a small cottage at the edge of the forest.

"Enough of the chatter." Ingrid got up after dinner and piled the plates in the sink. "I mustn't keep you up, for you need to rest. You have got a long day ahead." Perhaps a reminder that her hospitality was limited for Germans, however much they pleaded their innocence.

"Let me do that." Gerlinde took the sponge out of Ingrid's hand and began to wash the dinner plates. When the older woman protested, Gerlinde said, "It's the least I can do."

Lotte wiped up and put the kitchen and sitting room in order while Ingrid stoked the fire and threw their uniforms onto the burning heap. The fire crackled with violence as it devoured the dirty cloth. A single tear slipped down Lotte's face.

A chapter of her life had been closed past recovery. However much she had hated the Nazis, the war, and even her role in the Wehrmacht, it had been an essential part of her life. She'd already shed her skin once, becoming Alexandra Wagner; now it was time to molt again. Her life as Alexandra would soon be nothing but distant history, as she returned to her true identity of Charlotte Klausen.

But first she had to find her family.

She smiled, wondering what Ingrid's verdict about her real name would be. The odd woman certainly had some insight into life not everyone had. She might not be a witch from a fairy tale, nor a fairy godmother, but she did pick up on things between heaven and earth that most people were oblivious about.

Rex barked and Ingrid sat up straight, her hand grabbing at the rifle that was never out of reach. Beady-eyed, her posture straight and ears perked up the same way Rex's were, she listened intently to whatever danger might be lurking out in the shadows.

The dog gave a whimpering howl and she smiled. "All right, go out and catch your food." She opened the door for the dog and when she returned to see the girls facing her with mouths gaping wide open, she said, "Don't stare at me like that. Must have been a marten. No use in having them around, and Rex has to eat, too."

They finished their chores and Ingrid showed them to a tiny room upstairs, full of photographs from happier times. A young Ingrid in her wedding dress, obvious joy making the bride's face glow. There were other photographs of the couple and their son through the years, documenting their time together.

Lotte felt like she was peering into someone's secret life, but Ingrid wasn't embarrassed or upset when she noticed Lotte's interest. Instead she explained with a faraway look on her face, "My Arne was a keen photographer and I was his favorite subject."

"These are memories to cherish forever," Lotte said. "It is what keeps us united with our family, even when we're far away." The remorse over not having recovered her own family photographs stabbed at her heart. At least she had the single headshot of Johann, looking quite dashing in his uniform with the new stripes after his promotion to Leutnant during their time in Warsaw. In times of war, promotions were plentiful – for those who stayed alive.

Sadness crept into her heart and she suddenly felt Ingrid's calloused hand on her arm. An electric current shot through her and she felt quite a strange reassurance to keep on her path. The green eyes of the old woman shone with a brilliance Lotte had rarely ever seen, her own green ones paling in comparison.

"He will come home, my dear, but you can never give up hope and yield to his demands."

Whatever does this mean? Before she could ask, Ingrid's eyes clouded over and she jerked her hand away from Lotte's arm. The compassion in her voice turned into a cold business demeanor. "The bed is small, but so are the two of you. I will wake you at dawn and show you the direction of home. Good night."

"Good night," Lotte responded, but the older woman had already fled the room, closing the door behind her back.

"What was that about?" Gerlinde asked, her eyes wide like saucers.

"Honestly, I have no idea." A sudden chilliness took hold of Lotte, as she tried to understand the ominous words Ingrid had uttered. Was the old woman certifiably insane or did she know more than she should?

Always one to stand with both feet in the middle of life, usually in some kind of trouble, Lotte did not believe in the supernatural. Gypsies, palm reading, Tarot cards, all of that was only a fluke. The stuff of con men intent on pulling money out of gullible people's pockets. She shook her head. *Definitely insane.* Anyone living out here all on her own with only a dog as company would start seeing things that weren't there and talking in riddles.

CHAPTER 18

The ill-fitting and old-fashioned garments pretending to be dresses might look ugly, but they gave Lotte and Gerlinde a sense of freedom and confidence they had missed clad in their Wehrmacht uniforms. Wearing headscarves, they looked like any of the country folk that swarmed the roads.

They walked along the main road and hoped to reach the border within two days. The scorching sun, though, made the walking arduous. When a horse-driven cart passed close by, Lotte wanted to stop it and beg a lift.

"But what should we say?" Gerlinde, the voice of caution, said. "We'll never pass as Danes. We don't even speak Danish!"

"We could say we're German refugees on our way home."

"Can't wait to see all the goodwill that's gonna bring us." Gerlinde pursed her lips in a sarcastic smile.

They didn't have to find out, because their hesitation had taken too long and the moment was lost, the carriage fading away into the distance. Their fatigue increased with each step as the day got hotter. It was so warm that they removed their scarves.

To distract herself from the oppressive heat, Lotte struck up a conversation with Gerlinde. "What do you want to do once we're home?"

"I don't have a home, remember?" Gerlinde was in no mood to converse, but that wouldn't deter Lotte.

"Assuming you find your family, where would you like to settle down?"

"Any bloody place that's not in ruins, has no bombs raining down and certainly no soldiers around."

"That'll be hard to find." Lotte giggled, and finally Gerlinde stopped moping and smiled at her.

"Well, if we really can't go back to East Prussia, I think I'd like to live in Hamburg. It's a big city, close to the sea."

Lotte shook her head. "Me, I'll want to stay in Berlin."

"What's your obsession with Berlin, anyway?" Gerlinde wiped the sweat from her forehead. "Don't you want to return to Cologne?"

"Too many bad memories." Lotte quickly said. She had never been in Cologne, except for passing through to her basic training as radio operator. But Alexandra had supposedly lived there all her life.

"We haven't made much progress," Gerlinde said. "At this rate it will take forever to cross over into Germany. Ingrid said the only checkpoint open to Germans is near Flensburg."

Lotte groaned. That meant crossing the Danish peninsula from west to east, adding another forty miles to their journey. "We really need some kind of transport."

An unladylike snort escaped Gerlinde's lips. "And court danger just because you're in a hurry? That's a foolhardy plan."

"Do we still have some food?" Lotte asked, mulling over the request for a plan.

"Not much." Gerlinde distributed the rest of their bread. "That's it."

"See? We need to cross the border fast."

"Because on the other side there's milk and honey flowing?" Gerlinde rolled her eyes.

"No, but I guess we could work for food…"

"We can just as easily do that here."

"Didn't you just say yourself that nobody in this country likes the Germans, so why would they give us work?" Lotte kicked a pebble with her sturdy shoes. Brown, inelegant, a barbarous fashion sin, she had complained about the army-issue half-boots since she'd received them last year. But after walking for days, she actually thanked Oberführerin Littman for the graceless things.

"I know!" Lotte yelped. "We could pretend to be deported Jews returning home."

"You can't be serious." Gerlinde stopped in her tracks, her mouth hanging agape. "I don't want to pass as a Jew. How can you even suggest such a misbegotten thing?"

"Misbegotten? What are you talking about? They're people like you and me. In fact, I once had a friend—"

Gerlinde heaved in a breath. "You have Jewish friends?"

"Your jaw will dislocate if you don't close it." Lotte said dryly. "I had no idea you're such a fervent Nazi."

"I'm not a Nazi." A flush crept up Gerlinde's cheeks. "But Jews are just... greedy money makers... they keep all the best positions for themselves and control finances every chance they get. I didn't like that they were putting them into the ghettos, but it was a necessity. The Jews were destroying our nation."

"And they succeeded, right? Look what they did: they started the war, bombed our cities, killed millions of soldiers by sending them into a lost battle – oh, and don't forget the casualties they caused with their SS and Gestapo thugs," Lotte said in a derisive tone.

Gerlinde hunched her shoulders, looking outright miserable. "Of course not, but…"

"But what? What did they do to harm our country? Nothing… it was that bloody bastard Hitler who did all of this. I know, because I was…" Lotte didn't finish her sentence, because her friend gave her *the look*.

"Shush. If someone hears you…"

"See what the Nazis did? We just lost the war and you're still shushing me, looking over your shoulder, afraid a black-uniformed man with the skull on his lapels will jump out from the hedge and massacre us for what I said?" Lotte snorted.

"I'm sorry… it's just…" Gerlinde didn't have to explain, because they both knew all too well the realities they'd lived with for the past twelve years. She sighed. "I simply don't like the Jews, and certainly can't pretend to be one of them."

Lotte shrugged. If she had ever believed that the end of

the war would miraculously make everything better, now she had evidence it wouldn't. If even a kind and gentle person like Gerlinde had been indoctrinated to harbor such deep-running hatred, how could forgiveness come to this fractured world?

In silence they walked along the road, each annoyed by the other's remarks. With every step Lotte felt the tension between the two of them growing, and with it the certainty that the repercussions of the Nazi ideology would ravage her country for years, if not for decades to come.

Maybe Ingrid wasn't a case for the mental asylum, but she appeared to know things others did not. The lost war was not the end, but only the beginning. The beginning of filling up the abyss that had swallowed Europe along with its humanity, culture, compassion, and worst of all, future.

For the future looked bleak.

Am I like that? Lotte played football with a pebble. *Do I espouse prejudices that I am unaware of or hatred for something that is too deep-rooted to recognize?*

After a while, Gerlinde turned around and put her arm around her friend's waist in an effort to demolish the barrier growing between them. "Forgive me. I didn't mean to upset you. You remember those Poles in Stavanger they had doing the hard construction labor? Maybe we could pretend to be displaced persons from Poland?"

Lotte leaned against Gerlinde. "But how? My Polish is abysmal, you know that."

"Mine is fluent. Nobody will notice." Gerlinde smiled. "In the unlikely event that we actually come across a Pole, you just keep your mouth shut."

"Oh. So your proposal is just a ruse to keep me silent, while you chatter away all you want?" Lotte giggled with delight. She had hated the short time she was at odds with her best friend.

"Well, yes. So what do you say?"

"I say it's a plan."

CHAPTER 19

The afternoon dragged on and they passed fertile green meadows where Gerlinde would pick the odd edible plant, but Lotte's stomach continued to grumble.

"We need to buy food," she said.

"Do we even have money?"

"Some Reichsmark hidden away in my shoe, those should get us at least a decent meal."

"But we have to find a town with a shop first." Gerlinde paused for a moment, shielding her eyes from the merciless sun.

"After that godawful winter, who knew it could become so hot up here?" Lotte wiped the sweat from her forehead with the back of her hand.

"We're at the height of summer, when the days are endless. It's only normal for the weather to be hot." Gerlinde laughed. "It shows you're a child of the city, the likes of you never pay attention to the passing of the seasons."

"Oh, I did…" …*live on my Aunt Lydia's farm for two years.*

It was increasingly difficult for Lotte to keep her web of lies straight. Maybe she should tell her friend the truth about who she really was? But after their falling out over the Jews, she feared Gerlinde would abandon her when she discovered the truth.

"I don't want to walk anymore!" Lotte cried out, flopping to the ground. "I'm dusty, thirsty, hungry and my feet are aching. In fact, there's not a single cell in my entire body that's not in pain."

Gerlinde settled beside her, taking off her shoes and stockings, exposing feet covered with oozing blisters. "It was your idea in the first place. We should have stayed where we were. Eventually we would have been processed and released. At least we wouldn't be thirsty and going nowhere in the sweltering heat."

"Processed? Was that what you call being processed?" Lotte looked at her friend aghast, just as a military truck passed by, jostling soldiers included. She glared at the men and snarled, "Would you rather experience *that* again?"

"No," Gerlinde replied, hanging her head and looking away.

Lotte squeezed her hand. "We just need to get a ride. It shouldn't be that far to the border crossing at Flensburg anymore." To tell the truth, she had no idea where they were, since their only guide was the sun now hanging in the sky behind their backs.

They took up their journey again and when another horse-drawn cart passed, Lotte pushed Gerlinde forward to ask for a ride. The driver turned out to be a young Danish boy of about ten years of age.

His initial suspicion soon faded away when Gerlinde

told him they were Poles, forced to serve the German soldiers as their maids, and were now on their way home.

"Hop on," he said and moved over on the box seat to make room for them. "I'm Jens. And you?"

"Agnes and Maria," Gerlinde quickly answered, and after seeing Lotte's questioning glance, she specified, "I'm Agnes and my friend is Maria."

"Nice to meet you." Jens cracked his whip in the air, and Lotte involuntarily ducked her head. Another remnant from her time in Ravensbrück. Would she ever be able to function like an average human being again?

The horse trotted at a brisk pace and the miles rolled by. The inquisitive driver asked all kinds of probing questions, reminding Lotte of her nephew Janusz. Janusz had just turned thirteen, but he still had the annoying habit of every keen child to ask a million questions a minute, most of them starting with *why*.

"You have traveled a long way," the boy said. "I can take you about fifteen miles further south, where I have to deliver this coal."

"That's so kind of you," Lotte was grateful for the offer that would save miles of legwork.

About two hours later, Jens stopped at the marketplace of a small town and dropped the women off.

"Good luck," he shouted after them as he drove away.

Lotte looked around the sleepy village and found a bakery open. The owner wasn't too pleased to find out they would be paying with Reichsmarks, but he seemed to value the sale more than his pride and took the out-of-fashion currency.

When they stepped out of the bakery with freshly baked,

mouthwatering Danish bread, Lotte looked at the brooding darkness of the sky. Dark clouds had been rolling in from the west all day and were now piling up above the small town.

"I sure hope it won't start raining right now." Lotte walked to a bench at the side of the marketplace, where they bit hungrily into the hearty bread.

"Hmmm, that smells so good." Gerlinde closed her eyes in delight, sniffing at the warm, aromatic loaf in her hand. Just when they finished eating, the skies opened up and it began to rain, drenching them to the bone within moments.

There was no cover nearby, so they ran toward a row of houses and dove for shelter in a doorway, the torrential rains lashing down on them, soaking their clothes and chilling the girls.

"What a sorry end to a splendid day," Gerlinde said through chattering teeth.

"Can't have everything," Lotte trembled as she wrapped her arms around her. "Thanks to Jens, we have covered a lot of distance today. We should be able to get to the border crossing in a day or two.

"First, we have to find somewhere to spend the night," said Gerlinde miserably.

Lotte glanced at the torrential downpour and sighed. "I'm not going anywhere in this apocalyptic weather."

Gerlinde laughed. "What do you know about apocalyptic weather? That's normal near the sea. Sunshine one moment, rain the next. But the good thing is, it passes just as quick as it starts." Gerlinde's words proved true. Half an hour later, the rain subsided into a feeble drizzle, the wind pushing the dark clouds further east. The sun peeked out between ruptured clouds, conjuring up an enchanting rainbow across the sky.

"How beautiful," Lotte said, still shivering. "I'd love to go to the end of the rainbow one day and find the pot of gold."

Her friend giggled. "I'll come with you. But now let's go and find a place to stay for the night."

Looking like drowned cats, the two women were walking indecisively along the streets in the small town when they came upon a fishmonger's shop. A woman changed the sign from *open* to *closed*. She had her blond hair braided around her head and wore a blue-and-white-striped apron over her dress. She hung the apron on a hook, stepped out of the shop and locked the door.

Her gaze fell upon the two younger women and she said, "You got yourself quite wet. Do you have a long way to home?"

"Ma'am. In fact, we are a seeking an inn to spend the night," Lotte said in German.

The other woman's smile disappeared, replaced by a hateful stare, and she made to walk away.

"Please, we are Poles."

The woman tilted her head, studying the two girls. From close up, she looked to be in her late thirties. Neither her fashionable dress nor the rosy glow on her face, that was definitely assisted by skillfully applied cosmetics, could hide the wrinkles etched into her face.

"Poles?" she repeated, her red lips pursed. "And what brings you to this forlorn place?"

"We were kidnapped by the Nazis and brought years ago to work at the harbor in Stavanger, Norway, and now we're on our way home. We've been walking most of the way from Hirtshals." Lotte said, "But today a young boy gave us a ride on his horse-driven cart."

"That must've been Jens."

"Yes, ma'am."

The expression on the woman's face warmed. "There's no inn in this village. But how could I send you away after you've suffered so much? Come with me. I'm Karen, by the way." She extended her hand.

"I am Agnes and this my friend Maria," Gerlinde explained. "We can't possibly accept your hospitality."

"Of course you can. We are all travelers on the road of life," Karen replied. "If we don't extend a helping hand to those in need, we are worth nothing."

They followed her during the five-minute walk to a small house at the end of the village. Giving her friend the once-over, Lotte grimaced, throwing up her hands at the sight. They were both drenched, dirty, and presented a pathetic, bedraggled sight. Their dissimilarity to the elegant lady couldn't have been more pronounced.

Karen followed Lotte's gaze and smiled. "Take off your boots. The rest we'll take care inside."

Leaving the mud-caked boots and her stockings in the hallway, Lotte traipsed barefooted into the cozy home. Karen lit a cigarette and waved them onward.

"You'll catch your death like that. Go to the laundry room and take off your wet things. Give yourself a good wash and I'll fetch towels and something dry to wear for you." Karen disappeared and returned with two dresses. The one Lotte received was a black short-sleeved dress in A-line form with fancy white and pink birds printed on skirt and top. It was wide around the waist, but Lotte didn't care.

Gerlinde's dress turned out to be even fancier: a fiery red one with the same A-line skirt, and a pronounced corset-like waist with three decorative buttons on each side. The sleeveless top had a low bustline going way beyond decency, the décolleté thinly veiled by an inset of a half-transparent black material with white polka dots.

"Wow. You look stunning!" Lotte said and Gerlinde couldn't resist giving a twirl. Her skirt flew wide and stripes of the same polka-dotted cloth from the bustline became visible inside the folds of the skirt.

Lotte wondered where on earth Karen had managed to buy these two stunning dresses, when everyone else had to make do with ration coupons and mending old clothes. They left the laundry room and caught the appreciative glance of their hostess.

"Ah, look at you girls. So young and beautiful," Karen said, amazed by the transformation brought about by soap and water. "Hair like spun gold! All this loveliness hidden under...,"

"Layers of dirt," Lotte admitted and the three women laughed at the veracity of that remark.

"Well done. Now you look like peachy girls and not like tramps." Karen drew from her cigarette and offered, "You want one?"

Lotte politely shook her head, but Gerlinde all but jumped at the vice she'd missed so much these last days.

The hospitable woman told them to wait on the sofa in the sitting room and shortly thereafter returned from the kitchen with two steaming mugs and a plate of *smørrebrød*.

"Coffee, but not the real one. I hope you don't mind," Karen apologized.

"Not at all." Mind? Lotte had long forgotten the smell and taste of real coffee and she had definitely not expected such a luxury from her hostess.

"Where are you going?" Karen suddenly asked.

"Returning to our home town near Königsberg," Gerlinde truthfully answered. What she didn't mention was that area had once again changed hands and had been divided between Poland and Russia.

"That's quite a long ways. And you have to cross our neighbor to the south. It won't be nice. I hear the Allies have bombed all of Germany to ruins and there's no means of transport, no housing and even less food. Serves them right."

"Yes, we have heard this, too," Lotte said. Then, hoping to glean more information asked, "Do you know anything about the border crossing?"

"Not really." A wave of sadness overtook Karen's expression. "There's a checkpoint about twenty miles from here. Queues are long, because military traffic has priority and, you know, most people don't have proper papers. So they need to go to the British admin first and apply for temporary papers and a travel pass. It seems quite easy for the ones who only want to go a few miles into Germany, but if you want to cross occupation zones it gets really tough.

"For now, it seems the Allies have decided that everyone has to stay in the sector they were in when the war ended, but exceptions and inter-sector travel permits are given on a by-need basis. To go to Poland... I don't know. You'd have to talk to the Brits and then to the Soviets."

Lotte hadn't expected the traveling to be so complicated. Somehow she'd assumed they'd simply cross the border and be on their way. But upon closer consideration, they couldn't even use their Wehrmacht ID cards and thus were undocumented aliens, having to apply for some kind of temporary identification. She sighed.

Karen gave her a sympathetic look. "I know, I know. Isn't it a shame? But if you're not in a hurry, I can ask around and organize papers for you. It'll take only a few days and will make the border crossing a lot easier. Although I would ask you to work for me in the fishmonger's meanwhile. God knows I could use some help."

Gerlinde and Lotte exchanged a look. Both women actually were in a hurry to find their loved ones, but this offer was too good to pass up.

"That's a very generous offer and we certainly will work at your shop for the time being." Lotte said.

"We're used to hard work," Gerlinde added, and Lotte elbowed her. Neither one of them had any experience with fish, or with hard work. Tapping out Morse code might require plenty of focus, but it certainly didn't count as physical labor.

"Then it's a deal. How wonderful!" Karen was a cheery, good-natured person, in spite of her ebullient exterior with elegant clothes and too much make-up. But she also had a shrewdness to her and seemed to be able to organize anything – fancy dresses, abundant food and even identification papers. Lotte wondered how a fishmonger had come to be so resourceful.

Karen appeared to be delighted at having company and the girls soon found out why.

"My husband was a fisherman. He died years ago in a fierce storm. God bless his soul."

"My condolences," both girls murmured in unison. At least her husband hadn't died at the hands of one of their countrymen.

"Well, at one time we had four trawlers and a thriving fishing business, but now… it's not easy for a woman to keep those fishermen at bay." Karen gave a crooked smirk. "But I manage well enough, supplying our herrings to the military."

Now Lotte had a surprisingly good idea where the fancy dresses and the abundance of food came from.

"Don't judge me, girls." Karen pursed her lips, apparently aware of the hidden thoughts. "It's not that I particularly liked the German occupiers, but we all have to make do. Selling my merchandise to those who can pay proved beneficial – for me and those fishermen employed by me. With so many livelihoods at stake, what can a woman do? The resistance is a luxury pursued by the rich or the young, not by normal people like you and me."

Lotte nodded her agreement. In this war everyone had supported, appeased, or collaborated to some extent, and who was she to judge? Her own contribution to the downfall of Hitler had been minimal at best. And the time spent supporting the regime with her work – even though it served as a disguise for her spying activities – had probably been at least equal to Karen's actions.

Karen continued to talk, "Now the Germans are gone and the British are here. They, too, need to feed their army. So I continue to sell to the new powers that be. One day, when Denmark is free again, I will find me another man and sell only to Danes." She giggled at her own words. "More coffee?"

"No thank you, Karen," Gerlinde said.

"Now, I'll show you girls where to sleep, because we need to be down at the harbor before dawn when the ships come in." Karen clapped her hands and showed them into a spare room. The room was furnished with a broad bed. A colorful counterpane covered two thirds of the bed's length, revealing immaculate white sheets and the softest-looking cushions with equally white covers.

Lotte sunk into the soft mattress, Gerlinde by her side. Already drifting away into sweet dreams, she wished it was Johann sharing the bed with her, instead of her friend. What wouldn't she give to hold him in her arms again, showering kisses on his familiar face with the warm and alert eyes.

I wonder if he'll still have me after... after... She couldn't even think the words. She decided never to tell him, and in her dream the awful thing never happened. She stood at the platform when his train arrived and he climbed down, looking as dashing as ever, grinning down at her, before he swooped her up into his arms, kissing the breath from her lungs.

CHAPTER 20

Working in the outside shed alongside Karen – smoking, fileting, and canning the fish in oil – Lotte and Gerlinde became herring experts. Baskets of herrings were delivered daily by a stocky, bearded man, who returned in the evening to pick up the canned produce. It was a smelly business, but the women did not enter the house after a workday without taking a refreshing shower in the attached bathhouse.

But at the end of the week, when Karen paid them their wages, they were ready to move on.

"Have you heard about our temporary papers yet?" Lotte asked their employer.

"Not so fast." Karen laughed at her. "Things have their own speed in this sleepy town. But the mayor promised me to have travel permits ready for you before Sankt Hans Aften on Saturday."

"Sankt Hans?" Gerlinde asked.

"Don't tell me you didn't know. What have you girls learned during your time in Denmark?"

"I'm afraid not much about Danish customs," Lotte replied.

"Midsummer is the longest day of the year." Karen clapped her hands with glee. "And in Denmark we're celebrating it on June 23rd, which is the evening before Johannis Day. Now that the occupation is finally over, it will be a celebration like no other."

"Oh..."

"You'll have to stay until after the holiday. I urge you to join the local people in rejoicing and having fun. It'll be a worthy conclusion to your stay with us." Karen kept on talking, and in spite of her homesickness, Lotte became excited about the festivities that Karen painted in the brightest lights. Since it made no sense to leave before receiving their travel permits, they decided to stay.

Together with Karen, they arrived at the town square, where everything for the bonfire had been prepared. The heap of wood and straw was topped with a straw witch dressed not in the customary old women's clothes, but in a torn and ragged Wehrmacht uniform, holding a Swastika flag in her hand.

"This year it'll be special," Karen said, her eyes sparkling. "Summer solstice is a night imbued with evil, when the witches make their way to the Brocken mountain for their yearly reunion. But this year we're not only warding off the broomstick-riding witches and their evil troll companions, no, we send all the dastardly Nazis away with them."

The bonfire was lit, setting the sky above the village ablaze.

"Karen was right." Gerlinde stared open-mouthed at the enormous glow. "That's one big bonfire for sure."

Lotte watched the spectacle half-shuddering, half-rejoicing when the flames licked at the straw witch, devouring the Wehrmacht uniform and finally the Swastika flag until nothing but ashes remained.

The scorching depicted a befitting image of the state of her nation. And she had not even seen it with her own eyes, except for the newspaper photographs in Karen's house. More and more ugly truths had come to light.

Her first reflex was to deny – *that* couldn't be true. But of course she knew it was. Nothing she hadn't experienced herself as a prisoner in one of the concentration camps herself, albeit on a much smaller scale. The sheer amount of industrialized efficiency in the so-called extermination camps, which had been well-oiled killing machines, shocked even her.

In Ravensbrück the prisoners had been humiliated, exploited, starved, worked to death and treated worse than dogs, but their sole reason for existence hadn't been to be killed. She gagged, vomit filling her mouth. Looking around at the jolly crowd she almost doubted her own sanity, hoping, praying, this was just a harrowing nightmare.

A handsome young man with the blondest possible hair and ice-blue eyes came up to her and pushed a beer into her hand. "To our liberation!" he said in Danish and cocking his head with doubt at her incomprehension, again in German.

"To your liberation!" Lotte smiled at him and indulging his questioning glance, explained, "My friend and I are Polish slave workers on our way home."

"Welcome to our town."

An effervescent giggle erupted behind her and she turned around to see Karen.

"I see you've already caught the attention of a young fellow." In that moment a band began to play, and Karen said, "It's time to dance. I'll hold your beer."

Lotte shook her head. "I'm afraid I don't know any of your dances."

The fellow looked crestfallen, but Karen wouldn't have any of it and all but shoved Lotte into his arms saying, "You have to dance. It's Sankt Hans after all, and when can we be joyful if not tonight? I'm sure this lad will lead you masterfully across the dance floor, won't you?"

He dutifully nodded and wrapped his arms around her shoulders, leading her to where other couples were already dancing. "My name is Christian, by the way."

"Maria," Lotte answered. Despite her reluctance, she enjoyed the dancing and let him swirl her around not for one song, but until the music stopped. Every now and then she swirled past Gerlinde, who'd been swooped away by a dapper-looking man in a police uniform. With her cheeks flushed with exercise and the heat emanating from the bonfire, Gerlinde looked truly happy for the first time since they'd left Stavanger – even if only for a few short dances.

When the music stopped, someone raised her voice to sing and soon everyone fell in. "*Vi vil fred hertillands, Sante Hans, Sante Hans.*" We want peace in our lands, Saint John, Saint John.

Who didn't, after six years of harrowing war?

True to her promise, Karen presented them the next day

with temporary papers and travel permits, signed by the mayor of the town in the names of their Polish alter egos. With one sad, and one laughing eye, they said goodbye to their gracious hostess, who dabbed secretly at her eyes, before she said in a boisterous tone, "I wish you safe travels, and find yourself a good fellow to keep warm."

Then Karen handed them a loaf of bread and boiled potatoes for each of them and sent them on their way.

"It was nice to stay with her," Gerlinde finally said.

"Yes, but it's also nice to go home."

"If we even…"

Lotte shook her head, making her friend stop mid-sentence. News from Berlin was bad. It seemed the Russians had full control and wouldn't let anyone in or out, not even the other victorious armies. "A broomstick sure would help," she quipped, trying to lighten the mood.

"Yes, imagine the commotion when we fly into the cordon on our brooms, landing swiftly in front of the Brandenburger Tor," Gerlinde replied jokingly.

"Why not make it a noteworthy entry and fly through the gate instead?" Lotte held her side, erupting giggles making it hurt.

"Sure. And then we step down from our broomsticks and wait for the red carpet to be rolled out."

"If it's a red carpet to welcome us and not the anti-aircraft flak, we can call ourselves lucky witches." And just like that the gay silliness evaporated.

Lotte rubbed her nose, frowning. "First we have to get to the border, though… and cross it."

"We have papers, so there's nothing to worry about."

"I know, but seeing all the British soldiers about makes

me nervous." It was true. Every time Lotte spotted a uniform, a queasy feeling settled into the pit of her stomach. They were in Denmark on borrowed time, and it wouldn't take a Sherlock Holmes to find out their true identities.

Escaped prisoners of war.

In Nazi Germany those used to be shot or worse.

CHAPTER 21

Several miles down the road they came across a man fixing a tire on his rickety cart, which was more like the frame of an old truck minus the engine. The back was piled high with furniture, suitcases, and bundles, all covered with a large old tarp. His two sturdy horses grazed nearby while his wife and three children sat to the side, waiting for the job to be completed.

"Good man, are you going toward the border?" Lotte asked.

"None of your business," the large, barrel-chested man replied gruffly, barely looking up from his work.

"We are heading for Flensburg," Lotte persisted, and his head came up, looking at her with suspicion. She hastily added, "...on our way to our home in Poland."

"Poland, eh?"

"Yes, good man. We've been abducted by the Nazis to work for them and now we're desperate to get home and find out if our families are still alive." At least half of her sentence was true. Since adopting her new identity as Alexandra, lying and cheating had become second nature to her, but from experience she knew that it was always best to stick to as much of the truth as possible. Keeping up a maze of elaborate lies and remembering what she had told to whom had proven quite challenging.

"We have no room for passengers." His overgrown eyebrows knitted together in a frown.

"Please, we weigh very little and will not take up much space, if you could find it in the kindness of your heart to give us a lift," Gerlinde pleaded with him.

"Hans, look at them. Wouldn't you want someone to help them out if they were your daughters?" his wife suddenly said, patting the white blond head of the child next to her.

"Alright," he sighed, checking the knots on the tarpaulin. "Climb up and find space in the back. This covering has to remain because of the rain."

"God bless you and your family." Gerlinde was already scrambling up the cart, looking for a spot to curl up in.

"Hold tight, we don't need no delays," he shouted as he got into the front seat with his family, slapped the reins, and uttered a loud clicking command. The horses snapped to attention and began a steady trot. Lying comfortably on bundles, the two women couldn't believe their luck, counting the miles rolling by, each one bringing them nearer to their destination.

"It was a good time staying with Karen," Gerlinde said. "I miss her already. And look at the beautiful dresses she gave us."

"We'd never have gotten this ride if we were in the

ragged, dirty sacks Ingrid gave us," Lotte said, looking at the bright red dress Gerlinde wore, the one Karen had offered her friend the very first day.

"Right?" Lotte said. "Karen's care got us here, no doubt about it. We'll raise a glass to her one day."

"Speaking of drinks, that midsummer festival was more fun than I've had in years." Gerlinde laughed brightly and Lotte remembered the sparkling, fun-loving person her friend used to be.

"Oh yes, it was. I had forgotten that such things as a normal life still exist."

"It was good of Karen to insist we go with her." Gerlinde had a wistful, dreamy expression on her face and Lotte suspected it had something to do with the dashing young man in the police uniform.

"Karen sure is a very generous person. A bit peculiar, but with the kindest of hearts." In the beginning Lotte had judged the woman for her *very good* relations with the British officers, and probably with the Germans before them. But soon enough she'd accepted that every human had to make their own choices during difficult times. And while Karen might linger on the loose side of morals, she had a kind heart and generously shared the proceeds of such *work* with anyone in need.

In the evening they reached the small border town and thanked the driver and his family for the ride. It was too late to cross the checkpoint, so they bought some food and then took shelter in the empty train station for the night.

The next morning they took up their walk to the border checkpoint, a bigger lump forming in Lotte's throat with every step she took.

Gerlinde, though, didn't seem to feel the same, because her face brightened the nearer they got to the border control. "We're finally here. Can you believe it?" Gerlinde squeezed her friend's hand.

"It's hard to believe this is real," Lotte said staring at the border crossing, willing away the knot forming in her stomach. She had been pondering whether to tell her secret to the border guard, but remembered the brush-off by the base commander. No, it wouldn't do any good. "What should we say?"

"Say?" Gerlinde stared at her without understanding. "What do you mean? We show our papers and cross."

Lotte felt her face pale. "But what if they ask us something?"

"Then we answer their questions. What could they possibly ask of us?

"Oh, I don't know. Maybe, 'Are you escaped POWs?'"

Gerlinde laughed out loud. "You worry too much. Nothing will happen, you'll see. We're just two girls traveling home."

There were lines of people at the checkpoint, waiting to be processed. Men, women, and children. Young and old, in various conditions, assembled at the gate to pass into Germany, but most of them were German POWs, marched across the border into some prison camp.

Lotte turned her face away, afraid one of the men might have been in Stavanger and recognize her. It wouldn't bode well with the Tommies if the man lacked enough sense and called out her name, a name that didn't match the one on her temporary papers.

British military police manned the checkpoint and

seemed to give only cursory glances to everyone wanting to enter Germany. Only young males were scrutinized more thoroughly, and every once in a while one of them was led away inside.

Gerlinde elbowed her and whispered, "Look at that handsome lad."

Lotte followed her gaze to an officer standing right behind the two uniformed soldiers manning the checkpoint. He seemed to be some kind of supervisor, overseeing their work. And indeed, he was handsome. Tall, with broad shoulders, his uniform sported an array of ribbons, and coveted decorations. Cropped dark blond hair peeked out from under his beret; his face, although battle-hardened, still showed boyish features and Lotte guessed he couldn't be more than twenty-five years of age.

When his gaze fell on her, she quickly cast down her eyes, but it was too late. He'd caught her staring. Beneath her eyelashes she noticed his lips curving up into a bright smile that lit up his clear blue eyes. Lotte felt herself blush under his stare and fumbled with her hands.

"Go. It's our turn." Gerlinde shoved her forward and they showed their temporary papers to the soldier in charge, who only nodded and asked, "Going where?"

"Danzig," Gerlinde answered.

"Pardon?"

"East Prussia."

The young man glanced up and looked at them. "That's in Poland; why would two beautiful girls like you even go there?"

Again, it was Gerlinde who did the talking, since Lotte was still too embarrassed to look up, afraid she'd again meet the eyes of the handsome stranger standing behind the border patrol. "We are Polish and want to go home."

The young soldier shrugged and stamped their papers. "Here you go. You'll have to get new travel permits once you cross into the Soviet sector."

"Thank you," Gerlinde said in her sweetest voice, taking Lotte by her elbow and pulling her forward. Lotte followed her with wobbly knees and took a deep breath only when they passed the border patrol hut.

They'd made it.

"Excuse me, ladies," a deep voice said, and Lotte stared right into the face of the handsome officer who'd stepped away from his vantage point overseeing the crowd of travelers and now blocked their path. "May I see your papers again?"

His words punched Lotte's stomach as if he'd used his fist and she caught her breath, doing her best not to double over.

"Of course, officer." Gerlinde handed him her ID and the travel permit and Lotte somehow commanded her hands to do the same.

"I'll have to ask you to come with me, please." He uttered the fatal words with the most pleasant smile on his face, motioning for them to follow him.

He took them inside the building next to the checkpoint and to a small office with one desk and three chairs. After asking them to take a seat, he closed the door and leaned against the edge of the desk, towering over them. For a moment Lotte was transported back to the interrogation room in Warsaw, where the man questioning her had been with the Gestapo.

She knew her eyes had given away the fear when the man in front of her showed a lazy smile.

"I'm Sergeant Davis. May I check your luggage, please?"

Lotte cursed the fact that they hadn't replaced the stolen British army-issue kitbag with a more inconspicuous bag, but handed it over to him without delay. He quickly unpacked all their belongings, putting them on the desk one by one.

"Where is it?" he demanded to know.

"Is what?"

"Black market goods. We're looking for smugglers."

"Sir, you are mistaken, we aren't smugglers. We're just two girls on our way home." A huge burden fell from Lotte's shoulders. Smuggling black market goods was the one thing they weren't guilty of.

He peered intently at them, his expression not giving anything away. "I am never mistaken. You are cunning. But I know you are smugglers. I promise, I'll find the contraband sooner or later, so save us some trouble and tell me where you're hiding it."

Davis pulled the kitbag inside out and, ostensibly frustrated with the lack of finding incriminating evidence, he suddenly paused. "Where did you get this bag?"

"A British soldier gave it to us," Gerlinde said.

"I doubt one of our men would ever do such a thing." A sarcastic smile pursed his lips and under different circumstances Lotte would have admired him for his bright intellect and his cat-and-mouse play. But right now, terror threatened to consume her and strike her mute.

"We found it on the road and assumed the owner was dead," Lotte said.

He tried to smile but it ended up more like a sneer. "Picking over the bones. This is not getting any better for you."

"Oh no... we found the kitbag, not the owner..." Gerlinde stuttered.

Sergeant Davis seemed amused, but his next question came sharp as a whiplash. "What are you doing here?"

"We were kidnapped and the Nazis forced us to work for them." Lotte repeated their cover story.

The man snorted a laugh. "Slave workers? What kind of *work* did the Nazis expect from you in these fancy dresses?"

Gerlinde flushed beet-red and started protesting, but he waved her protests away.

"I prefer a whore over a smuggler any time of the day," he said with an appreciative smirk that made Lotte's skin crawl. "Why don't you show me a sample of your skills and I'll let you go?"

Fear morphed into cold rage. Did all men believe women had been put on the face of the earth for the sole reason to please them? "We certainly won't. We're decent women."

"Decent women?" He guffawed. "Last time I checked neither smuggling nor whoring was on the list of decent occupations. So what's it gonna be?"

"I want to talk to your superior, Sergeant Davis," Lotte blurted out before she could think her request through. It might not be the wisest course of action, since she and Gerlinde teetered on thin ice, but she would not endure *that* again. She preferred to be court-martialed – did they even do that to escaped prisoners of war?

Davis looked insecure, but only for a fleeting moment.

"And what do you want to tell my superior? That you were caught stealing British Army property and want to evade your just punishment?"

"I believe even in England just punishment for alleged stealing doesn't include sexual favors." Lotte had no idea where her sudden strength came from, but she steeled her spine and with her cold stare dared him to contradict her.

"You can pack your things," Davis said, returning her stare.

While the women packed their belongings into the kitbag, he turned their papers over again, dissatisfied with his lack of finding the black market wares he'd been so confident were inside it.

Lotte gave a hidden sigh of relief when he opened the door and told them to follow him. In the hallway some soldiers in British uniform lingered, smoking. Lotte had taken English classes in Stavanger and thought she managed the language quite well, but she understood less than half of their banter. Sometimes it seemed like a different language altogether.

Their heads turned as Gerlinde passed them in her bright red dress, and Lotte now wished they'd put on Ingrid's sacks instead of Karen's fancy clothes. It was like running the gauntlet under the leering eyes of the young men. One of them catcalled after them, followed by a word Lotte didn't understand.

Gerlinde, though, turned around and stared at the offender with her coldest, aristocratic, disdainful expression, the one she'd probably perfected on their Polish farm hands back home in East Prussia.

"Don't stare at me like that, peachy miss, I've done nothing wrong," he said, sporting a huge grin.

"You very well know that is not a word to address a lady," Gerlinde replied and turned on her heel.

"What word? Oh? You mean *ślicznotka*? Do you understand Polish?"

"They claim to be Polish refugees," Sergeant Davis said, a lazy smile traveling across his face.

Lotte froze with fear, because she saw the sliver of hope in Davis's eyes and feared hearing his next words.

"Maybe you'd like to have a chat with your compatriots, Andrzej? Finding out what they're really doing up here?"

Lotte all but choked on the lump forming in her throat as she imagined herself in front of the firing squad.

Gerlinde squeezed her hand and whispered a barely audible "Let me" before she gave the Polish man her brightest smile and asked in Polish, "Where are you from?"

A conversation between the two of them ensued that none of the others understood.

"This one's clean," Andrzej said, all smiles and then addressed Lotte. "*Dzień dobry, panienko.*"

She was busted. With no idea what he had said, she preferred to nod and smile.

"My friend is frightened." Gerlinde excused Lotte's silence. "We grew up together and I can assure you she's no smuggler either."

"Not a smuggler," he guffawed. "But not a Pole either." He switched to Polish and asked, "*Jak się nazywasz?*"

Lotte gave her best guess. "Danzig."

Judging from the horror reflected in Gerlinde's eyes it had been the wrong answer.

"Danzig? That's quite an unusual name for a girl. So tell me, do you actually speak any Polish at all?"

"No." Lotte sighed; her only remaining option was the truth. "I'm not really Polish. I just tagged along with my friend."

Sergeant Davis grinned like a child on Christmas Day. "I knew it. You are under arrest."

CHAPTER 22

Lotte and Gerlinde were brought to separate cells, where they had to undress down to their undergarments. Lotte didn't care anymore that the young soldier saw her in her unmentionables, because much to her horror he searched her discarded clothes and found her Wehrmacht identification. After being ousted as liars and Germans, there wasn't much to be saved anyways.

"Look at this." He gave a low whistle at the sight of the treasonous document and handed the dress back to Lotte. "You can get dressed again. I'll take this to Sergeant Davis."

After an endless time biting her nails she was brought to Davis's office.

He waited for her with a happy smirk on his face. "Told ya. My instincts are always right. You two struck me as suspicious from the moment I saw you standing in line at the border control."

She couldn't help but contradict him. "Not exactly right, though. You thought we were black market smugglers."

"Okay, I'll give you that one. You're not a smuggler; you're even worse. A Nazi trying to evade captivity. That's a major crime and I can assure you my superior will be extremely pleased – at me, not at you."

"And again, you're wrong." Lotte despised his obnoxious, arrogant behavior so much she had to rub it in. To hell with the consequences, she was done for either way. "We're not evading captivity, we escaped it."

The hardened expression in his blue eyes told her not to continue down that route and she hastily added, "We got separated from our transport near Gram and since we were too afraid to return, we decided to try and get home on our own."

"You and your friend?"

"Yes." She sighed. "It probably wasn't the wisest thing to do, but believe me, we had our reasons."

Lotte struggled to inhale, whether it was because of her fear, or the dingy, confined space, she didn't know. After their confrontation Davis had sent her to an interrogation room. For him, the job was done and now the trained interrogators would try to squeeze the truth out of her.

A large soldier entered the room and sat down heavily, the chair squeaking in protest at his hefty bulk. He looked at her with beady eyes, asking question after question.

Lotte answered them as best as she could, trying to keep as close to the truth without admitting to the details about their escape and what had happened before. He wouldn't believe her anyways and if he did, he probably wouldn't mind – might even get ideas.

"Your friend has told a different story," he said without any forewarning.

Shocked to the core Lotte hissed in a breath, racking her brain over what Gerlinde could have said differently.

"The way I see it…" he made a long pause, boring his steely gaze into her, making her go numb with fear, "… you're a Werewolf."

"What?" Her eyes popped wide open and the numbness left her body with one furious stroke at the mention of the legendary, mysterious, and dreaded underground organization that had been founded by Heinrich Himmler himself.

"You heard me right. We believe you're part of the Werewolf organization, intent on criminal activities and sabotage of the victorious powers."

"I'm no such thing!" she all but yelled at him. "I was a radio operator in the Wehrmacht, putting messages into Morse code. That was all I did."

The corners of his mouth tugged upward. "And when the war was over, you slipped into your new role as spy for the Werewolf organization."

Her shoulders slumped. This man wouldn't believe a single word she said. And he had every right to distrust her. An innocent person didn't fabricate a false identity and spin a web of lies.

"You know what happens to German spies, don't you?" He threw his head back in a gesture of belligerent power. "You will be executed. Would you prefer the firing squad or would you rather be hanged by the neck?"

"You can't kill me without a proper trial." Her voice came out weak, even to her own ears.

"I can and I will. Who's gonna stop me? Your friend? Your almighty Führer? He committed suicide, if you care to remember."

"So, you're intent on doing the very things you are prosecuting the Nazis for? What about my human rights?" she protested, exhibiting courage she didn't possess.

"Really? You dare to talk about human rights? We didn't run death camps and gas chambers, unlike you Nazi swine." The man looked at her through eyes filled with animosity strong enough to knock the breath from her lungs. "We'll teach you a lesson you won't forget. I promise you that."

Lotte shuddered, remembering the unforgettable lesson from Gram.

"Do what you will," she sighed and slumped into her seat, exhausted by all the questions and threats. They should just end it with her. Make it quick and painless. Her mind wandered. If he was serious about her choosing her own execution method, which would she prefer?

Not hanging. The mere thought of struggling for breath tied her stomach into a nervous knot. And the image of her feet dangling in the breeze for everyone to see and point fingers at her. *Nazi bitch. Good that she's dead.* No, definitely not hanging.

Firing squad. A bullet straight into her head and eternal blackness. Instant oblivion. It sounded reassuring, but what happened if the soldier missed the target and instead hit her lungs? Choking her slowly to death? Or her stomach – God forbid.

The guillotine. The sharp knife was precise. And fast.

But did the British even use it? Or was that only the French during their revolution? Suddenly, she was embarrassed at her lack of history knowledge. Her brother Richard, he would know. Before being drafted, he'd driven her nuts with his habit of always sticking his nose into a book. *Richard would know which execution method to choose.* She scoffed at her own morose thought.

"You are finding this funny?" her interrogator asked.

"No, sir," she answered, tilting her head. "Just trying to figure out which way I'd prefer to be murdered by your lot."

His jaw fell to the floor, too shocked by her disregard of his threats to form a coherent answer. He simply bored his brown eyes into her, as if he could suck the life from her body by willpower alone. When he finally found his voice again, he said, "You will confess. They all do in the end."

Then he strode from the room, leaving her alone with her thoughts. She broke into a crazy sobbing giggle at the cruel irony of fate that she, a spy for the British, would soon be executed because they'd accused her of being a spy for the Germans.

When the giggling sobs subsided, she inhaled deeply, wondering whether she should have told her interrogator that she'd been the one giving them the codes to decipher her messages week after week?

She'd been about to blurt it out more than once, but had restrained herself every time. There was no reason to believe he'd buy into her story. He might not even know about these kinds of operations, since it had all been top secret. Every agent had been but a spoke in the wheel, knowing only her own part and her contact person. Nothing more.

Lotte herself never knew what Lina did with the codes. Whom did she give them to? How did they find their way to London?

No, her story would never fly. Too far-fetched it seemed, too much evidence against her, and – most accusatory of all – too desperate. They'd think she made everything up as a last resort to avoid execution.

Later, Sergeant Davis returned, greeting her with a smug smile on his handsome visage. She couldn't really blame him, since he'd had the correct gut instinct to mistrust her and Gerlinde, but nevertheless she wanted to wipe the arrogance from his face. What did he know about her reality?

"Can I have something to drink, please?" she asked.

"No, you cannot. Not until you confess."

"There are regulations…"

He waved her complaint away. "This is a holiday camp compared to how you Nazis kept your prisoners."

"I'm not a Nazi," Lotte protested weakly.

"Sure. You're not a Nazi. Same as I'm not a British soldier." He didn't listen to her mumbled protest, talking himself into a fit of rage. "Suddenly, no German has been a Nazi ever! Nobody knew anything about war crimes, atrocities in the camps and whatever else your lot has been hiding from the world. But I was there, liberated the POW camp in Fallingbostel. You should have seen my captured comrades…" His handsome visage distorted into a grotesque grimace. "Living skeletons they were, not more than skin and bones. So starved, some couldn't even stand on their own feet."

His fist came down onto the table in a violent slam and she shrieked.

"You know what else I saw?" His clear blue eyes clouded over with so much pain that Lotte instinctively put a hand across her heart.

"Nobody prepared us for this infernal sight." His voice became soft and thick with emotion. "It was surreal. Inhumane. We marched up to a camp at least four times the size of Fallingbostel. Later we found out there had been fifty-three thousand prisoners when we opened the gate – men, women, children. Most of them Jews. They didn't resemble humans at all." Sergeant Davis openly sobbed for several moments, before he found his voice again. "I'll have nightmares my entire life from seeing the atrocious crimes your people committed. Even after we liberated the Bergen-Belsen camp, the former prisoners kept dying from the effects of their ordeals. I swore that very moment that I'd avenge every last soul murdered, tortured or otherwise abused by the Nazis."

The conditions in a concentration camp weren't new to her, but she gasped at the mention of Bergen-Belsen. Her sister Anna had been able to find out that Lotte's friend, Rachel, and her baby sister, Mindel, had been deported to Bergen-Belsen in 1943.

"You have the gall to gasp!" Davis yelled at her, the introspection disappearing from his eyes, replaced with utter hate and the ardent yearning to hurt her as much as the Nazis had hurt their prisoners. "Don't tell me you didn't know."

"I knew alright, I was…" Of course she knew, she'd been imprisoned several months in one of the camps, but he wouldn't understand, probably wouldn't even believe her if she told him. He'd made up his mind, judged her as a despicable Nazi, a guilty perpetrator to be punished. Nothing she said would sway his mind.

What had happened was far too cruel to cope with. In order to live, one had to dissociate oneself from those who'd been capable of such monstrous crimes. Sergeant Davis had chosen to label all Germans as Nazi monsters.

She couldn't even blame him for it.

"I'm sorry," she said.

He looked confused, his blue eyes loosing the steely hardness. "Why are you sorry if you claim you did nothing wrong?"

Yes, why?

"I'm not apologizing for what I personally did, but I'm truly sorry that all of this happened. That millions and millions of people had to suffer and die in this godawful war. And I'm sorry that I was much too young to do anything about the first signs... not that it would have made much of a difference."

For the first time since she'd met Sergeant Davis, there was appreciation in his eyes. He blinked and then asked, all business, "Why are you here?"

She sighed. She'd told the other soldier her story at least ten times. That she was a Wehrmachtshelferin, worked as a radio operator in Stavanger, Norway. That all females had been evacuated via Denmark when it became clear Germany would lose the war. That she became a prisoner of the British after the surrender.

"Why did you escape?"

Lotte shrugged. "I told you before, we got separated from out transport and decided to make our own way home..."

The door opened and another soldier came in, giving Sergeant Davis a bunch of papers and murmuring some explanation to them.

Davis turned to her and said, "Your friend told us a different story. So, who's telling the truth?"

"How should I know, since I have no idea what she said?"

The lazy smile curling Davis's lips made her aware she'd given herself away.

"I mean. I'm telling the truth, but maybe Fräulein Weiler elaborated on other details of our ordeal." It was as weak an excuse as they came.

"She says you both escaped from a British camp at Gram. And here," he tapped on one of the sheets of paper, "you're listed as absconders."

"So yes, it's true. I escaped. You would have done the same." Lotte stared at him, feeling the rage snaking up her spine. How could he change from compassionate man to arrogant asshole in a matter of seconds? "Hasn't your own army given the directive that it is every captured soldier's duty to escape?"

"That was true when we were still at war. Now it's different. Your country surrendered unconditionally so you have no duty to escape. We're the ones in charge now. And we can do with you as we please. We can even shoot you for running away."

Lotte's blood boiled, but she hid the trembling from her voice and said as calmly as she could muster, "We had our reasons for escaping, reasons that have nothing to do with my country and everything to do with my dignity."

"Your dignity?" He gave an ugly chuckle. "If it were up to me, I'd rip that dignity from your body, trample on it and then feed it to the hungry wolves. That's what you deserve. All of you. Monsters."

Seeing the futility of this argument, the fight left her body and she gave a deep sigh. "You're right. And that's exactly what your comrades did. They stole our dignity when they forced themselves on our group of women."

She saw a shadow in his eyes, but it disappeared within an instant and he pushed his chin up when he said, "At least you weren't gassed in the shower. Should have just relaxed and enjoyed it.."

Lotte's fingers twitched as she thought about how delightful it would feel to scratch out his eyes, no doubt bringing retribution of the worst kind. Thankfully, the door opening distracted from her plan and two men led inside a visibly shaken Gerlinde.

Davis strode from the room with his mates, leaving the two women alone inside the sticky room. Gerlinde fell into Lotte's embrace, both of them drawing strength from the nearness of the other. When she heard loud voices outside, Lotte let go of her friend and inched closer to the door.

"What we gonna do with them?" one of the soldiers asked.

"Boss said we have more urgent problems than two Fräuleins."

"We could let them go."

"They deserve to suffer, after everything their people did."

Lotte pressed her ear against the door, listening intently to the discussion behind it, hoping they would come to the conclusion that two girls weren't worth wasting more of their time.

"That dark-haired one, he said they'd return us to Gram," Gerlinde whispered.

"Shush. I'm trying to listen to what they say," Lotte responded, straining her ears again.

"We could give them a fright, threatening a court martial before we let them go."

"We might find a better use for them, though. It's been a while, could do with a shag."

Lotte blanched when the conversation took a randy turn and each of the soldiers tried to outdo the next one with his ideas of a great fuck.

"What are they saying?" Gerlinde asked.

"I can't really understand," Lotte lied, unwilling to share her burgeoning fear with her friend.

They waited miserably for quite a while before the door opened and four soldiers appeared inside. Sergeant Davis wasn't among them and his absence probably meant the men didn't come in an official role. But Lotte wasn't sure whether this was a good or a bad sign.

"Guess what I have here?" One of them waved some papers at the women. "Your discharge papers and proper travel passes."

Lotte stretched out her hand, but he held the papers high above her head, his face a teasing grin. "You can have them alright, if you show us your gratitude and a good time first."

It took her a minute to process his request and she scrunched up her face in confusion, certain she misunderstood his words.

"I'm not that kind of girl." Gerlinde blushed with embarrassment.

"Aw, what's the big deal?" he asked. "We don't ask for anything you haven't done before."

"It won't be to your harm," said another. "We'll show you some good fun."

"Think about it, you'll be on your way home before tonight. We even put in cigarettes and food for your trip." The dark-haired soldier laughed as if no self-respecting woman would ever refuse his truly generous offer.

"You lassies will enjoy it. What do you say?" The man with the papers in his hand looked at the women with a sly grin as Lotte felt her stomach flip over.

While Gerlinde seemed to shrink with every raunchy comment, Lotte gathered the remnants of her courage and wrapped them around her like a cloak of protection. A fuse blew in her head, jumbling her thoughts into a mass of outrage. She had endured too much during this war to continue being a victim. "And you claim higher moral grounds for your lot? Where's that British respectability now?"

"Come on, no need to insult. We just want a quick shag, so it will do all of us some good. Call it understanding among nations…" The soldiers snickered at his joke.

But Lotte didn't care about keeping calm anymore. If she had to lie down, she'd do it kicking and screaming. She deliberately let her anger erupt like a volcano. Her words spewed out like molten lava and she couldn't care less about the consequences of her outburst. Nothing could be worse than what they were expecting of her.

"You are disgusting pricks!" Lotte shouted at them. "You are the people who are supposed to restore right and order. Is this your understanding of morality? A bunch of rotten cowards is what you are, taking advantage of defenseless women. Can't you take it up with someone your size? Bloody assholes!"

When she saw their reaction, a little of her bravado faded away. Her slur to their manhood didn't go down too well with the soldiers. The dark-haired one who seemed to be the tough guy in the crowd glared daggers at her and turned in a swift move to squeeze her breast.

Gerlinde's begging glance urged Lotte to stop antagonizing the men, but Lotte snarled like a wild animal caught in a trap. She wouldn't go down without a fight, even if defending her honor was the last thing she did in this life.

Remembering the brawls with her brother in her youth, she responded to the unwelcome touch with a swift knee to his groin. The man doubled up, moaning in pain.

"Shoot the bitch!" he gasped. "Don't let her get away with attacking a British soldier."

His call to his brothers in arms was immediately answered and the next thing Lotte knew, she was caught in a vicelike grip, the muzzle of a pistol jammed into her neck.

"This is the way you want to go, is it, lass?" the man holding her hissed.

She sensed his hot breath on her neck, and heard Gerlinde begging for mercy. Lotte, though, had never begged for mercy in her life. Not even when she'd faced a firing squad. She wouldn't start now.

"I'd rather die than pleasure a dick like you," she bellowed. It was a bluff. Staring death in the face, she'd do just about anything to survive. But she counted on his not shooting her in the interrogation room with so many people milling about in the hallway outside the door.

CHAPTER 23

"Not worth the trouble shooting these bitches, lads."

Tears of relief filled Lotte's eyes as the man holding her stepped back and lowered his pistol. She unsteadily straightened her back, her gaze falling on Gerlinde, who stood against the wall, her eyes round and nervous red dots heating her cheeks.

She wanted to walk over and comfort her friend, but thought it prudent not to move, lest the tension in the room stirred again and one of the agitated soldiers did something everyone would later regret.

"Yeah, Eddie, not worth the bother, mate." His pals slapped him on the back and walked him out, breathing an audible sigh of relief. The situation had escalated way over their heads and neither the soldiers nor the two women had known how to get out of this self-created mess.

Just seconds after the door closed, it opened again and the soldier who'd kept silent all throughout the upheaval returned, giving them a stare that was difficult to interpret.

"You'd better come with me, before something else happens."

Lotte nodded, and she and Gerlinde followed him like the sweetest puppies to a cell. As soon as he had locked the door and they were alone in the cell, Gerlinde turned around, glaring daggers at Lotte. The normally gentle woman trembled with unabated fury and pointed her index finger at her friend.

"You! How stupid are you, Alex?" Gerlinde's voice turned into a high-pitched shriek. "I told you to keep your big trap shut, but no, you had to mouth off. You nearly got yourself killed. And me too!"

"I'm sorry." Lotte hunched her shoulders, intensely studying her toe-caps.

"Look at me, when I'm berating you! What were you thinking by provoking them? I'm sure we could have sweet-talked them out of their proposal, but no, you chose to insult their manhood. Don't you have the slightest idea how to deal with a man?"

"I guess I don't."

"Never in my life should I have embarked on this crazy adventure with you. I'm done with you and your antics." Gerlinde's shoulders sagged and she turned her face away, making the guilt flow over Lotte with a surge of power.

"Please don't think that way." Hot tears pricked the back of her eyes and she couldn't hold them back. Her friend meant the world to her. And now her weakness of character – the one she had believed she'd conquered – had caused a rift in their friendship.

For years Lotte had worked so hard to keep her bull-headedness under control. She'd vowed to think first and do later, to always ponder the consequences of her actions and never act rashly again. And once again, she'd lost her wits and had steamrolled over the soldiers, making things worse – for everyone.

"Forgive me. It will never happen again, I promise." Lotte took a step toward Gerlinde, but her friend backed away.

The tragic expression on her friend's face sent a pang of regret through Lotte. "Oh, Alex, will you never learn?"

"I have learnt my lesson." Lotte protested. "I will never put you at risk again or get us into trouble. I'll make it up to you. I'll get us out of this. I promise."

"Sometimes I don't know who you are." Gerlinde sighed deeply. "I see this stranger and she scares me."

Lotte shivered from the impact of Gerlinde's words. *You truly don't know who I am. Because I'm not Alexandra Wagner. There's so much I want to tell you but can't.* For a moment she hesitated, ready to spill the beans and tell her friend everything. The whole sorry truth of the mess her life had become. Starting with the stint that had sent her straight into a concentration camp, the fact that she'd been a spy for the British – the same army she had been running away from since Gram.

It was useless to try and make her understand. Gerlinde didn't possess the gene of rebellion. In contrast to Lotte, she never felt the urgency to strive for justice, the overwhelming need to fight for those who couldn't fight for themselves, the enthusiasm to do what was right. Lotte shrugged, abandoning the desire to bare her soul.

"What now? Thinking about your next misdeeds?" Gerlinde asked with such a tired tone it only fortified

Lotte's decision not to tell the sordid truth. Not now anyway. She'd wait for a more suitable opportunity. When they weren't holed up in a cell and when Gerlinde wasn't spitting mad at her for almost causing their demise.

In the evening, the guard brought them food and they attacked the plates like hungry lynxes, ravenously devouring the contents. Their appetites sated, the women lay down on the two cots in their small cell.

"Promise you won't make it a habit to end up in a prison cell?" Gerlinde asked in a conciliatory tone.

"I promise." Memories of the time in Warsaw when the Gestapo had arrested her came flooding back to Lotte and she fondly thought of Johann, her knight in shining armor. She had loved him before, but after what he'd done for her then, she'd never stop loving him until the day she took her last breath.

"You don't happen to know someone who could rescue us, by any chance?" Gerlinde seemed to have read her mind.

"Let me check my address book and get back to you," Lotte said with a laugh, happy because Gerlinde wasn't angry with her anymore.

"Come on, ladies. You made quite the impression yesterday. Colonel Barber wants to have a word." The warden rattled the bars of their cell door. "Hurry up. You don't keep the boss waiting."

Lotte jumped from the cot, straightening her dress and finger-combing her hair even as she slipped into her boots and walked to the door. She couldn't have a bath and put on some clean clothes, but she wanted to look as presentable as possible. This Colonel Barber was probably poised to decide their fates.

Thus prepared, the two women followed the warden down the hallway with pounding hearts and sweaty palms. He led them into a large, furnished room that seemed to be the colonel's office. Moments later two soldiers from yesterday's fiasco entered the room.

"What are these two ladies accused of?" Colonel Barber asked, sitting at his desk.

The taller of the two soldiers nervously put a file down in front of his superior, and remained standing at attention with his comrade. The colonel scanned the pages of the file and looked questioningly at the two men, who stood straight as a rod, eyes ahead, feet together and arms at their sides.

"I heard there was an ugly incident yesterday, but these notes don't tell me much," Barber remarked, looking at the men over his glasses. "Perhaps you'd like to enlighten me, Private Briggs? I believe you were there and witnessed the event."

The men didn't move, but Lotte noticed the discomfort creeping into their eyes. One of the others must have snitched, or how did the colonel even get wind of what had happened? She'd expected them to keep their mouths shut tight, as their behavior hadn't been up to protocol. And judging from their sweat-covered foreheads they knew it.

"Well, sir, it's like the report states," the man called Briggs mumbled and jumbled his words as he tried to rush his explanation. "These two ladies became difficult and had to be restrained, sir."

"And you, Private Fallon?" The colonel fixed his piercing stare on the soldier who'd held his pistol to Lotte's neck. "Did you find these ladies challenging in some way that required the use of your weapon?" He glanced at the fragile women, who didn't look in the least bit threatening to a strong man.

"Yes, sir, out of hand they were, these two lasses." Fallon squirmed under the colonel's icy stare. "Look like butter wouldn't melt in their mouths right now, sir, but they were a couple of wild furies yesterday."

"I see. And it took four of you to subdue these two women?" Colonel Barber asked sarcastically.

"They're Nazi spies, trying to cross the border illegally. Told a pack of lies, they did. You can't believe a word they say, sir," Fallon answered.

"Please give Charlie a shout-out for three cups of tea, will you, Private Briggs?" the colonel instructed. "And remain in the room while I question the ladies."

"Ladies, what do you have to say in your defense?" he asked Lotte and Gerlinde, who stood quietly at the opposite side of the desk.

Now or never. This might be her only chance to make up for her rash behavior the day before.

"Sir, it is correct, we were German prisoners of war," Lotte spoke boldly. "Under the laws of the Geneva Convention, we must be treated humanely, with respect for our persons and our honor."

The three cups of tea arrived and the colonel took one and signaled Charlie to give the surprised women a cup each, while the men stood at attention in stunned, angry silence.

"You are quite right, Fräulein," Colonel Barber agreed. "Are you saying you have not received proper treatment?"

"No, Sir, we have not. The abysmal treatment at Gram was the very reason we escaped, to protect our honor and decency." She cast her eyes downward, partly because she was still ashamed at what had happened to her, but partly, too, to emphasize her point.

"I am sorry to hear this," he replied. "I will definitely make enquiries into your allegations. And now, perhaps you can enlighten me about what took place between you ladies and my men yesterday?"

"Ladies, my bloody arse! Lying bitches is what they are, sir. Nazi bitches," Private Briggs snapped. His contorted face flamed a bright red, and the veins on his forehead stood out like knotted vines.

"Private, you do have a flair for dramatics," the colonel cautioned his infuriated soldier. "Calm down and mind your language, as we have ladies present. Please proceed, Fräulein."

Lotte didn't waver under his scrutiny, pondering how to best frame the situation to make the Colonel sympathize with her and Gerlinde. She couldn't really rely on his moral code, because, although forbidden, forcing oneself on an enemy woman was considered a misdemeanor, a harmless offense that was better left unchallenged.

"Your soldiers entered the room and offered us discharge papers in exchange for sexual favors," Lotte answered before the courage could leave her. "We declined their offer in no uncertain terms."

"And that caused the entire commotion?" Colonel Barber asked with an amused smile.

Hot pangs of guilt reminded Lotte of her own outburst that had only served to aggravate the situation. "Not exactly, sir. I may have overreacted and called them names."

"Names? What kind of names?"

Her ears burning hot with shame, she glanced up and met the colonel's eyes. "Disgusting pricks," she mumbled.

"And that caused my men to restrain and threaten you with lethal force?"

Lotte steeled her spine. She'd dug this hole for herself and her friend, she had to climb out of it now. "Sir, I believe it wasn't until I called them a bunch of rotten unmanly cowards that they saw red."

He sat very still for a long minute before he spoke again. "My men certainly aren't cowards. They fought all the way from Normandy to Flensburg against the hideous Nazis. But that doesn't excuse excessive force and use of weapons." He seemed more amused than upset by Lotte's explanations. "They know I won't tolerate such behavior on my watch."

"She slapped me, first," Fallon said, trying to defend himself. But he only made things worse.

"Slapped you? A soldier in uniform? Well, that's a reason to strike back with your pistol." Colonel Barber raised one eyebrow, obviously toying with his men. "And why did she slap you?"

"Because he grabbed my breasts," Lotte answered quickly. "Yes, I slapped this man, because it was a shameful thing to do and a woman has the right to defend herself."

"Lies, pure lies!" Private Fallon looked at his partner and managed a weak laugh.

A small hand grabbed her elbow and Lotte turned to look into Gerlinde's pleading eyes, giving her the silent order to stay put. She gave her an almost invisible nod. She regretted her outburst yesterday and had promised to make it up.

"Women usually don't fight an armed soldier, especially not at the border control," Colonel Barber said.

"My honor was threatened, sir. I had to protest." Lotte half-heartedly defended herself.

"Honor?" Briggs intervened. "Escaped Wehrmacht auxiliaries you are. You left your honor in Gram, from where you escaped."

They had left their honor there, all right. But not because they had escaped. Gerlinde put her face in her hands, the shame of that day still haunting her.

"So, you are both escaped Wehrmacht auxiliaries," the colonel said. It was a statement rather than a question.

"Yes, we are," Lotte whispered.

"Enemy combatants on the fly. That doesn't sound good for you. We have a special punishment reserved for those who still oppose us. You know that, don't you?"

Private Briggs smirked and mumbled under his breath, "Hanged by your neck."

"Wait!" Lotte cried out. "It was all my idea. Gerlinde, I mean Fräulein Weiler, she had nothing to do with it."

CHAPTER 24

The piercing gaze of everyone in the room burned through her.

She couldn't be sure they'd really be hanged, but she wasn't willing to take the risk. The least she could do was to save Gerlinde.

"Please, sir, it's true. It was all my fault. I begged her to come with me. She didn't want to. Punish me, but let her go," Lotte pleaded.

"Is this true?" the colonel asked Gerlinde.

Tears shot into her eyes and she nodded. "Yes, it was Fräulein Wagner's idea. I tried to talk her out of it, but when I saw her determination I agreed to go with her. Couldn't leave her all on her own in a foreign country, now could I?" She tried a crooked smile. "So that makes me as culpable as her and I insist on being tried together with her."

"A pair of fiercely loyal Nazis who aren't trying to save their necks at the expense of someone else. That's a first for me," the colonel said.

"We're not Nazis…" Lotte stopped talking under the warning eyes of her friend, who hissed, "Don't make things worse than they are."

As if things could get any worse.

"I need to tie up a few loose ends, ladies." Barber flipped through the file, penning notes on the pages. With bated breath, nobody else in the room moved, waiting for his verdict.

He's hammering the final nails in our coffins. Lotte snaked her hand around Gerlinde's wrist, hoping to gain some strength from the nearness of her dearest friend.

"So you ran away from Gram, because you felt you weren't treated according to the Geneva Convention?" The colonel raised his head, his dark blue eyes boring into them.

"Yes, sir," Lotte answered.

"You know that fleeing was not the correct way to handle it? You should have reported whatever you felt was out of line. We have procedures in place."

Lotte balled her fists. Procedures. Reporting. As if that would ever lead to any results. Not in her lifetime. "Yes, sir. And we're sorry. We acted without careful consideration."

"So you admit that it was wrong to escape captivity and defy our authority over all Wehrmacht personnel?"

"Yes, we do," Gerlinde said. It was best to give the man what he wanted, in the feeble hope he might find it within himself to exercise mercy on them.

"And what about you?" Colonel Barber addressed Lotte.

A sudden gut feeling told her he appreciated a person who stood up to fight for what was right more than someone who merely obeyed orders. After all, hadn't every captured Nazi so far told the new powers that they'd only been following orders?

She was taking a chance, but it was worth it, if it saved their lives. Returning the colonel's gaze she nodded and took a deep, calming breath.

"Sir, yes, it was legally wrong to defy the British authority and escape, but sometimes a person must do what is morally right instead of following orders and rules."

The colonel's eyebrows shot up. "Explain."

"Since this war started I have done too many things that were against the law. I was never good at taking orders and when what I was supposed to do interfered with my personal ethics, I simply wouldn't do them." She kept looking at him, seeing the spark of interest awakening. Perhaps she could talk her way out of this situation. "Because of this character weakness, as my mother liked to call it, the Nazis sent me to a concentration camp for reeducation. You know what this entails." She let her gaze wander across the room, finding recognition in the faces of the soldiers present.

The colonel leaned back and tented his fingers. "Go on."

"I don't regret what I did; I just regret that I wasn't more careful in hiding it." She forced a chuckle. "After surviving this there wasn't much left that could scare me. But what happened in Gram... it was so outrageously unjust. Can you imagine my disillusionment when the very soldiers I had awaited for so long to liberate us from Hitler's reign, shredded to pieces my view of right and wrong? I couldn't sit idly by and let it happen again."

She paused for effect and then concluded her statement, "That is why I escaped, because your soldiers violated my sense of justice and I won't let this happen ever again. I'm not sorry that I defied the authority, because if I have learned one thing from this war, it is that you always have to act according to your sense of ethics. No matter what your orders entail."

The room plunged into stunned silence, barely a breath could be heard. Until Gerlinde broke the spell with a whisper, "You never told me you were in a concentration camp."

There's so much more I never told you about.

Lotte used the opportunity of a bathroom break to wash her face, neck and arms and bring her stubborn red curls into a presentable hairdo. Her black dress with the big white and rose birds looked the worse for wear, but she managed to straighten some of the wrinkles and wipe off the dirt with water.

"How do I look?" she asked her friend.

"Like the clean version of someone I thought was my best friend," Gerlinde pouted.

"Please, Gerlinde, I had my reasons for not telling you. It would have endangered your life, had you known."

Gerlinde pursed her lips and turned away. "Let's go. We shouldn't leave the colonel waiting."

Lotte sighed. Her friend's reaction was understandable, but there was nothing she could do now. The threat of execution still loomed over their heads.

Half an hour later they sat in the officer's mess with Colonel Barber, who'd – much to their surprise – invited them for lunch.

"Now, Miss Wagner, I admit, you surprised me with that enthusiastic speech in my office and I'd love to hear more."

"There's not really that much to say…" Lotte hedged.

He fixed his clear dark-blue eyes on her, a man who had seen everything and wouldn't be fooled by a pretty face. "I do believe there's a lot more to it. Or is this another badly fabricated backstory?"

"No, sir, it's not." Lotte shook her head to emphasize her words. "It's just… I'm not sure how much I'm allowed to say."

"Allowed to say? Now you really have my attention." He rubbed his clean-shaven chin, studying her intently. "Why don't you start with telling me how you came to be released from the camp – and why on earth did the Nazis later allow you to work in the Wehrmacht? That doesn't make much sense, now does it?"

Lotte almost giggled at the sheer ridiculousness. "Put that way, it really doesn't." She looked at the colonel and decided to come clean. To hell with secretiveness and half-lies. She might as well start with a clean slate into her new life – if she had one.

"I wasn't released; I escaped."

"Seems to be a recurring pattern." The colonel's eye filled with mischief, encouraging her to continue with her story.

"Afterward, I changed my identity and became Alexandra Wagner."

He nodded as if this was the most normal thing in the world to do. Gerlinde, though, let out a gasp and hissed, "You lied to me all this time?"

Lotte felt sorry for her friend, who had to find out in such a crude way, and whispered, "I'm sorry, but I couldn't tell you." Then she returned her attention to Colonel Barber. "One of the nuns in the convent where I'd taken refuge brought me into contact with a man who turned out to work for the SOE. He recruited me."

"He recruited you?" Barber's eyes snapped wide open and the fork filled with food in his hand stopped mid-air.

"Yes, sir. It was his idea that I join up as Wehrmacht-shelferin. I trained as a radio operator and gave the secret codes to decipher our messages to my contact person. First to the Polish Home Army, and later to the Norwegian Milorg."

"You were a spy for the enemy? A traitor to our country? How could you?" Gerlinde got up and stormed away. Two military police guarding the door to the mess caught her and, at a gesture from the colonel, took her away.

"What will happen to my friend?" Lotte asked, the food suddenly tasting bitter.

"Nothing. She'll be brought to the cell to calm down," he reassured her. "But I would ask the same question: What made you betray your Fatherland?"

"It stopped being my Fatherland when the Nazis deported my Jewish friend Rachel. I promised they would pay for it – one day."

"You're quite the rebellious lady," he said. "Let me verify your story. If it's true, I'll properly discharge you and your friend and arrange for travel permits."

"Thank you," Lotte said.

The rest of their lunch was spent with small talk about weather, food and the wish to return to their respective families.

She returned to the cell – for lack of a more appropriate

place – with a much lighter heart. The threat of execution was over, but she had to fight another and more important battle first: reconciliation with her best friend.

Gerlinde sat on the cot, arms around her knees, face dug inside the cocoon. Lotte slipped beside her and put an arm around her friend's shoulders.

No reaction.

"Gerlinde, please."

The other woman didn't raise her head, but at least she spoke, albeit in a grave voice: "You lied to me all this time."

"I'm sorry. It wasn't really lying. It was withholding information for your own safety. A matter of life and death."

"Why didn't you trust me enough to confide in me? We are friends, aren't we? We have been through the mill together, in Poland and here, and yet you continue to hide things from me." Gerlinde finally looked at her, her expression laced with sadness.

Lotte's heart wept at the raw agony she saw on her friend's visage. "I didn't want something horrific to happen to you because of *me*."

"Ah, you lied save me?" Gerlinde shrugged, her tone disdainful. "You know something, Alex? Keep your secrets. Quite frankly I don't want to know, nor do I want to remain in a so-called friendship based on lies and distrust."

"My real name is Lotte. Charlotte Klausen."

"I don't care!"

CHAPTER 25

Later in the afternoon, after a half-hearted reconciliation, they were taken to the colonel's office again. When they entered the room, he was sitting at his desk, conferring with Sergeant Davis.

Davis got up and extended his hand saying, "Looks like you were spies after all, just not for the other side. I apologize."

Lotte took his hand and shook it with a smile. "Your instinct was right." She didn't hold a grudge against him; he'd only done his job. And nobody could blame him for the hate he felt for everything German, not even Lotte.

They filled in routine paperwork to process their discharge from the Wehrmacht and receive new civilian IDs with the required stamp of the British authorities.

"Where are you headed now?" Colonel Barber asked.

"My family in Berlin," Lotte replied, quick as a shot.

Gerlinde, though, hemmed and hawed. "I have no idea

where my family is. They fled the Red Army in East Prussia."

"Sorry, but our own soldiers have yet to enter Berlin." The colonel's jaw was set tight. "I can't issue travel permits into the capital, and neither can I issue them for the Soviet zone."

"Do you have relatives in some other place?" Sergeant Davis asked.

Gerlinde just shook her head with a dull expression, but Lotte said, "Yes, sir. My aunt lives near Munich in Bavaria."

"Munich? Isn't that in the American zone?" Davis said.

Colonel Barber unfolded a paper with a map of Germany, neatly divided into four zones. Red for Soviet in the east of the country, green for British in the north, blue for French and yellow for American in the south.

"Indeed it is," he said, tracing his finger down to Munich on the southeast end of Germany. "It's a long ways from here. You sure you want to go there?"

"Yes, sir. I don't have anywhere else to go," Lotte said and after stealing a glance at her friend, added, "Fräulein Weiler can come with me if she wishes. I'm sure my aunt wouldn't mind."

"Well, then. I'll issue travel permits for the British and American zones." The colonel stamped several papers and handed them over.

"Thank you so much, sir," Lotte said as she glanced at her new papers, issued in the name of Alexandra Wagner.

He seemed to notice her hesitation and said, "I'm afraid we don't have any records of your original identity. This is something you'll have to fix once you find your family."

"I will." She smiled, a blessed wave of relief flowing over her.

"I can offer you a lift to Hamburg, but from there you have to make your own way. Hurry up to catch our transport, which is just about to leave. And take this, it should help on your trip." He offered them a few packages of cigarettes.

"Thank you so much, Colonel Barber, but we can't possibly accept this." Gerlinde protested even as she leered greedily at the smokes.

"You can and you will. I can't let our trusted spies go on foot, now can I?" He chuckled and shoved the cigarettes into Lotte's outstretched hand. She quickly slid them into her bag, giving Gerlinde a warning stare. The cigarettes represented a valuable currency and under no circumstances would she allow her friend to smoke them.

Hours later, perched on a crates of supplies in the back of an open-bed truck, they approached Hamburg.

"Oh… my… God!" Gerlinde said, watching the utter devastation around them. They had known it would be bad, had seen Flensburg, near the Denmark border, in ruins. Had passed the towns of Schleswig, Rendsburg and Neumünster, all of them nothing but rubble.

But nothing had prepared them for the infernal sight the formerly beautiful, majestic Hanseatic city presented. Nothing but debris, destruction and drabness. Lotte closed her eyes and remembered how beautiful Germany used to be at this time of the year. Trees dressed in bright green leaves to celebrate the summer. Now they were but bare skeletons against the sky, impoverished and pathetic. Like the people on the streets, the trees were cloaked in ragged garments, and none of Hamburg's past splendor existed to suggest even a shred of that grandeur.

What she couldn't close was her nose. The odor of rotting carcasses invaded her nostrils and she gagged. Opening her eyes again, she saw her own agony reflected on Gerlinde's face, deep wrinkles of sorrow etched into it. Nothing but misery greeted them. A world mostly devoid of able-bodied men; women stood in long lines, picking up brick after brick to clear the rubble from the ruins of the city.

"What a tragedy!" Gerlinde squeaked, unable to form more than those three words that stood for every awful thing they'd seen on their five-hour journey.

Only the children seemed content. Free of the constant threat of air raids or ground attacks they seemed as jolly as ever, running about the ruins playing hide and seek or tag.

"Stop, or I'll shoot!" A pre-school boy mimicked what he'd seen from the soldiers occupying his nation and his opponent dutifully raised his hand, grinning like a fool. "Now it's my turn." He pried the stick used as a pretend-rifle from his friend's hands and said, "Run!"

Lotte shook her head at the wondrous resilience of the youngest of her nation. After growing up amidst bombs and grenades they hadn't lost their childish ways, and playing in these war-ravaged surroundings seemed to be the most natural thing in the world.

"Not a place to stay in, girls!" the driver advised as he dropped Lotte and Gerlinde off near the central train station.

He was right. Hamburg was a broken city, reeling from the effects of conflict. The Allied forces' air raids had effectively obliterated the city. Gone were the large areas of parkland, and magnificent historic buildings, the boats on the Elbe River. Instead, an alien landscape confronted Lotte.

She blocked out the sight of city streets with scorched building facades cut up haphazardly by the bombs and firestorms as a sense of despair trickled deep into her soul. If Hamburg looked like this, how much worse off would her beloved Berlin be? The capital, the coveted prize of the winner? She'd heard on the radio that the Red Army and the last contingent of German defense – boys aged ten to fifteen – had fought a cruel and senseless battle in the streets of Berlin, tearing down what the bombs had spared.

Tears threatened to choke her at the pointless loss of so many young lives in the last days of a war that had already been lost.

"Let's take a train out of here," she said to Gerlinde, who seemed equally as shaken.

"But where to?"

"Anywhere but here."

Gerlinde turned around and looked at Lotte for a long time, the old habit of understanding each other without words returning, and she said with a deep sigh, "You're right. Let's find a place to stay for the night and decide what to do in the morning."

Lotte tried an uncomfortable smile. Gerlinde knew that Lotte had no intention of traveling to Aunt Lydia in Munich before she'd found her family. But her friend wasn't ready to pile another fight on top of a fragile reconciliation.

They walked into the train station but found that the

railway tracks were still damaged, so no trains were running.

Slow desperation took hold of Lotte and drained all the energy from her. They'd come this far, and now they would be deterred by some stupid railway tracks?

CHAPTER 26

"Don't despair," Gerlinde said and took Lotte's hand.

There it was again, the caring friendship they'd almost lost over the constant slew of lies Lotte had fed her friend.

Gerlinde dragged her friend behind, stopping every now and then to ask passersby about a place to spend the night. Finally, a young woman said her mother owned a small inn in a village outside Hamburg.

"I'm going there right now, and you're welcome to come with me. Not many paying guests these days," the woman told them.

"We would be more than happy," Gerlinde said.

Lotte could only stare with dull eyes. The desolate state of Hamburg had slashed her reserves, making her fold beneath the oppressive weight of sorrow for her family. She nodded to everything Gerlinde arranged, unable to voice an opinion of her own.

Today, she was happier than ever before to have a dear

friend to rely on. On her own, she'd have stayed at the empty train platform waiting for the railway tracks to be fixed in days, weeks or months time. Today she'd run out of strength and needed someone to take care of her.

The woman led them to a place where a horse with a cart waited. "Please hop on. This is our transport."

The old-fashioned horse-cart would have looked utterly displaced in the vibrant city of Hamburg less than five years ago. Now, it blended nicely with the gray and dull ruins of debris lining the street.

Lotte barely found the strength to climb atop and then slumped against the bench for the one-hour ride. She barely noticed when they arrived in good time in a quaint little village and stopped in front of an ancient cottage with an unbalanced appearance, but otherwise sturdy and surprisingly untouched by the mayhem that had engulfed Hamburg.

The innkeeper, Frau Konrad, was elated to receive guests and showed them a nice room with two big beds made of oak timber, a wardrobe in the same wood, two chairs and a small table. In one corner of the room was a white washbasin with running cold water.

Lotte bent down and let the cold liquid flow over her hands and forearms, splashing it into her face and on her décolleté. Slowly, her life spirits awakened again.

"Thank you Gerlinde, for taking charge," she said, offering her friend a one-armed hug.

"That doesn't mean I stopped being angry with you," Gerlinde answered, thin-lipped.

"I know. And I apologize again. I should have told you as soon as the war ended. But I was afraid you wouldn't understand, would hate me for lying to you…" She gazed at her friend and both of them started laughing.

"You were right. I hate you for lying to me."

"Don't hate me, please. I never meant to hurt you. But I was sworn to secrecy by those who helped me to escape from the camp."

"Why don't you tell me, how you escaped—" A knock on the door interrupted their discussion.

"*Herein*," Lotte said, relieved to postpone the explanation.

Frau Konrad peeked her head inside. "Is everything to your liking, *meine Damen*?"

"Yes, Frau Konrad. Thank you very much."

"At what time would you like to come down for supper? I have potato stew."

"Whenever it suits you best," Lotte replied, noticing a rumble in her empty stomach.

"Well, then, in twenty minutes would be fine." Frau Konrad closed the door and they heard the click-clack of her shoes going down the stairs.

"Let's get ready," Lotte said.

"I know what you're doing here." Gerlinde gave herself a cat's lick at the washbasin.

"What am I doing?"

"Evading my questions." Combing her long, blond hair, Gerlinde peered into the mirror and caught Lotte's eye.

"Alright, I'll tell you. Just not right now. It's difficult for me to remember that time in my life." Lotte sighed.

Gerlinde gave her a weary look, but didn't press the issue and, punctual like good Germans, they showed up downstairs in the restaurant attached to the kitchen. Frau Konrad's daughter carried a big pot of steaming hot stew to the table. A delicious aroma wafted through the room, making Lotte's mouth water.

Apart from them one old couple sat around the only table. They looked the worse for wear and Lotte wondered what horrible experiences they had witnessed. She didn't have to wait too long until the old man asked them where they were headed.

"Berlin," she blurted out, casting an apologetic glimpse at Gerlinde.

His face turned ashen and his wife's hands began to tremble. "It's not a place anyone would want to be in. Especially not pretty young ladies like you."

"I know about the risks," Lotte said. "But I have to go and find my family."

"You know nothing!" the old woman yelled, her eyes rolling in a crazed expression. Then she sank back against her chair, as if someone had hammered a nail into a tire and deflated it. "You have no idea!"

"We just escaped from there." The man explained his wife's behavior. "Nobody is safe there. People are starving. Women are… the Ivan is a monster. He has no shame or decency."

"You're probably right." Lotte had no intention of arguing with the old couple, especially when she could clearly see the devastating effect the conversation had on the wife. Changing the topic she said, "I've heard this area is prone to subsidence. Is this true?"

Frau Konrad, who'd just entered the guest room to remove the dishes, answered the question. "It is, *mein Fräulein*. This area sits on deposits of salt and the land is constantly shifting and sinking."

"Is that dangerous?" Lotte asked, almost laughing at herself. Who would worry about a bit of subsidence after five years of air raids? "Can we expect the roof to collapse while we're asleep?"

"No, of course not. The subsidence is gradual, it happens over centuries, so you have nothing to worry about."

Later, when they were each lying in their own bed, Gerlinde asked, "Wouldn't it be prudent to do as advised and go to see your aunt in the American zone? She might have news of your family. They might even be with her."

"First, I must find my sisters and my mother. Anna is a nurse and Mutter worked in an ammunitions factory. Neither of them would have been allowed to leave Berlin by the bastard who shot himself when things became dire." Lotte spit out the words.

"Shushh… if someone hears you."

"What then? The war's over and we're free to speak our mind again. At least as long as it's against Hitler. Not so sure about criticizing our new rulers."

"Alex… I mean, Lotte… everyone tells us Berlin is off limits. Can't you at least wait till conditions improve? In a month's time things might look different and you can go to Berlin without risking your life."

"You don't really expect me to take it easy and drink more tea?" Lotte grinned at the thought of herself taking up the attitude of a bored English noblewoman with a fine china cup of English Breakfast tea in her hand, the little finger extended *graciously*.

"There is no real tea on the market, if you haven't noticed," Gerlinde replied dryly, before she burst out in a fit of giggles. "And no, I can't imagine you sitting back and waiting."

"Please, come with me to Berlin." Lotte suddenly had the urge to make sure of the support of her friend.

Gerlinde sighed. "I'm not coming."

Deep inside Lotte had known the answer already, but it still hit her in the gut. Having to continue the journey on her own seemed so... daunting. Impossible, almost.

"Why?" she whispered.

"Because... I'm tired, worn out. I just want to take it easy and drink more tea. Make inquiries about the whereabouts of my family. And if I find out something, I'll travel to meet them wherever they are. Staying in the British zone, right here, near Hamburg is the best course of action for my plans."

"You could do this in Berlin, too," Lotte protested feebly.

"Do you even listen to what other people tell you? Since we left Stavanger every single person told us that Berlin is the last place on earth you should go. My family ran away from the Red Army, I'm not setting foot into the Soviet zone. Over my dead body."

Lotte understood Gerlinde's thinking, and she knew it was the rational thing to do. The safe choice. But where she was concerned, family loyalty was far more important than her own safety. Anna had sacrificed so much for Lotte, the least she could do was to try and find her sister now.

Gerlinde spoke up again. "Frau Konrad said I can earn my board working for her. And I'm free to travel to Hamburg when needed to make inquiries about my family with the authorities and the Red Cross. I'm sorry, but I can't come with you. I just can't."

Lotte heard her friend's labored breath in the darkness and she physically felt the guilt emanating from the other woman.

"Don't feel guilty. This is my choice. I hope you find your family."

"And I hope you find yours."

Saying goodbye the next morning was the hardest thing to do. They held each other for the longest time, knowing they might not ever meet again. With tear-filled eyes, Lotte waved back at the quaint little house until it faded from view.

"Don't worry too much," Lukas, a neighbor of the innkeeper, said to her as he drove his truck down the road. He worked for the British, transporting all kinds of goods to feed the starving population, and had offered her a ride about halfway to Berlin to the border with the Soviet zone.

"I don't," she lied, because she was scared to death after all she'd heard. In addition, she already missed her friend and, like having a limb freshly severed, she felt as if Gerlinde was still attached to her.

"We're here," he said, stopping the truck in a town called Schnackenburg.

Lotte bid her goodbyes, gritted her teeth and took off for the ferry across the Elbe River that separated the British from the Soviet sector. After all she'd heard, she'd thought it would be much harder to cross, especially since she still didn't have a valid travel permit for Berlin. The flimsy checkpoint at the ferry landing was manned only by two visibly drunken Red Army soldiers.

"*Schöne Frau, komm!*" one of them said with a heavy accent.

A shudder ran down her spine, so she was afraid to follow his order, *Come here, pretty doll*. But what choice did she have? There was only one way to cross the Elbe – swimming in the strong current was out of the question – and it meant she had to pass the checkpoint and board the ferry.

She mustered every last ounce of her courage and held her identification papers in front of her chest like a shield. The soldier took them with one hand and swiftly wrapped his other hand around her shoulders, pressing a slobbery kiss on her lips. Lotte stood stiff as a pole, swallowing down the bile in her throat and waited with growing terror for what would happen next.

"*Не здесь,*" the other soldier barked. Lotte was too terrified to hear what else he was saying. She understood the words *no* and *here* and wanted to weep with relief when he let go of her.

He gave his comrade an angry stare and an even angrier grumble, even as she launched for her papers in his hand. Then she dashed off onto the ferry, her heart thumping and her legs wobbly. As soon as she'd reached the safety of the boat, her knees gave out and she slumped against the railing.

An adolescent boy, thin as a rail, with dark hair and worn clothing hanging from him like a tent, approached her. "I saw what he did."

Lotte nodded, suppressing the need to retch.

"You were lucky they had work to do," he said.

She raised her head and looked into warm chocolate-colored eyes. The boy couldn't be older than maybe thirteen but he had the knowing eyes of an ancient man.

The ferry docked at the other side of the river with a bump, knocking Lotte off-balance. The boy grabbed her hand and didn't let go of it, even when she'd found her balance again.

"I'm Markus, and you?"

"Alex," she said, leaving her hand in his. Even though he was only a youth, it gave her the comfort of not being alone in this.

"You have a boy's name?"

"My full name is Alexandra." She smiled. "Where are you going?"

His face fell. "Berlin. I hope to find my aunt there, the rest of my family…" His voice became high-pitched and tears appeared in the corner of his eyes. Lotte squeezed his slender hand.

"I'm headed for Berlin, too. Should we make the journey together?" She surprised herself with the offer, since she'd known him for less than five minutes. But his childish face had looked so incredibly sad… and sweet. He wouldn't harm her. They'd be better off together.

"But not the way you're dressed," he grinned, nodding at her fancy dress. Despite wear, dust and dirt, Karen's dress still stuck out against the other travelers like a sore thumb. "Except if you want to attract the attention of the Ivans."

"Goodness, no!" she exclaimed. "But I don't have anything else to wear."

"Leave it to me."

They left the ferry hand in hand and walked into the

village on the other side. Markus seemed to know his way around, because he pulled her behind him to the cemetery.

Her heart thumped in her chest. "What are we doing here?"

"Finding clothes for you to wear."

Lotte shuddered and wanted to protest, but Markus had already dashed off and shortly after returned with dusty trousers, shirt and jacket.

"You don't seriously expect me to put on the clothes of a corpse?" Lotte retreated a step in disgust.

Markus giggled. "In fact, I do. Because we're going to make a man out of you. Now stop being so squeamish and change out of your dress."

She glanced at the boy who seemed to think this was a good idea, and a funny one at that. "Will you at least turn around?"

Another giggle left Markus's mouth. "Can I trust you?"

"You can," Lotte answered automatically, while she pondered whether she could actually trust him.

"My real name is Martha."

"M-Martha?" It took a few seconds to register in Lotte's brain. And then she understood. "Oh."

"You wouldn't guess it, now would you?" Martha beamed with pride. "I've crossed the Soviet zone twice in search of my family, and no Ivan ever bothered me. Not even once."

Lotte relented and changed into the suit that had belonged to a short man, but still bagged on her. If it weren't for the suspenders, she'd lose the trousers with every step she took.

"It looks great," Martha said. "But you need to keep the

jacket closed at all times, because your boobs will betray you."

Thankfully the jacket could have hosted two of her, and the unflattering garment hid every trace of her female curves.

"Now we just need to take care of your hair."

No sooner said than done. Martha fumbled a knife from her shoulder bag and Lotte closed her eyes in horror as she attacked her beautiful red curls.

"Done. Even your mother wouldn't recognize you." Martha put a hand over her mouth. "I'm sorry. Is she still alive?"

"I hope so. In fact, I'm going to Berlin to try and find her and my sisters." Lotte ran a hand, then two hands, through her hair – agonized, stupefied. Barely one inch of her formerly chin-length mop of hair was left. She probably wouldn't even recognize herself – if she had a mirror to check.

"We need to walk all the way to Wittenberge. From there I heard there's a train going to Berlin," Martha said with the authority of someone who'd been on the road for too long.

CHAPTER 27

Two days later Martha and Lotte arrived in Berlin and parted ways. Lotte retraced the familiar steps from the central station, Bahnhof Zoo, to the apartment building where her family had lived for decades.

But nothing was familiar anymore. She barely recognized the streets and got lost more than once in the endless catalog of obliteration. It was like the jaws of hell had opened up and swallowed the entire city of Berlin, leaving only molten vomit behind.

As she trudged the streets, she saw women queuing for rations, women removing debris from the ruins, women collecting stones to be reused, women layering bricks, women repairing tram rails, women driving buses.

What she didn't see were men.

Having lived surrounded by men in the garrison for such a long time, Lotte was amazed at the lack of countrymen. The only adult males visible were Allied soldiers striding along the streets as if they owned them – which, in fact, they did.

She stopped at a corner to ask directions of a tired-looking woman removing bricks with her bare hands. The woman stretched her back with a groan and looked at Lotte with dull eyes that had long lost their light. "Down there and then to the left."

Before she departed in the indicated direction, Lotte indulged in her curiosity. "Why don't you let the men do this backbreaking work?"

"Men? Which men?" The woman wiped the sweat from her forehead and murmured, "All dead, imprisoned or missing. You got lucky you're alive."

The old post office a block away from her building was obliterated, but the ancient linden tree in front of it stood defiantly like a headstone to mark the spot. How often had Lotte and her siblings climbed those sturdy branches when Mutter had to go into the post office to stamp her letters?

"It's unladylike for you to behave in such an unrefined manner. Why can't you be more like your sisters?" Mutter had scolded. Lotte continued her antics until that day when she was twelve years old and a boy whistled up at her.

"He can see your knickers, Lotte." Anna and Richard doubled up laughing. Lotte never climbed that tree again, though now that she wore the attire of a man she fought an irresistible impulse to scale those branches once more. Instead she ran her hand through her cropped hair and walked on, determined to be as resilient as that beloved old tree.

When she finally arrived at the building where her

family lived, the shock settled deep into her soul, impeding any movement. She stood frozen to stone on the street, a car honking at the obstacle she posed, her eyes widening by the moment. A barely standing structure with gaping bomb holes in walls peppered with bullet holes, and smashed window panes, confronted her. Where her apartment used to be the wall had a different color, as if freshly erected to repair a hole.

Please God, let them be alive and here. Lotte prayed, though in her heart she couldn't fathom anyone living in these conditions, especially Mutter, who was so fastidious about cleanliness and tidying her home.

She slipped through the entrance door that hung on the hinges. Rushing up the damaged stairs, taking three steps at once, she met a young boy dashing down. He brushed past her without a word, darted on outside into the street and disappeared.

Lotte's heart nearly stopped. He hadn't recognized her, but despite his having grown so much in the past year she recognized him immediately. If her nephew Jan was here, the rest of the family must be, too. With newfound energy she bounded up to the fourth floor and stood on the landing, heart thumping and palms sweating.

She banged on the door with both fists, not caring whether she alerted the entire neighborhood. Not even the neighborhood gossip, Frau Weber, scared her right now, because what would she do when the believed-dead daughter of her neighbors returned home? Denounce her to the new authorities?

"What the hell are you trying to do, you crazy boy?" Her

brother-in-law Peter opened the door, scowling angrily. The last time she'd seen him in Warsaw he was an impressive, fear-inspiring, burly man. Now she stared in shock at his hollow face and skeletal frame. His own clothes hung on him in as ludicrous manner as the stolen clothes hung on her.

Riddled with shock, she couldn't utter a single word.

"You want to break a door that's already hanging on its last hinges? We have no money, nor anything else. Go away." He attempted to slam the door in her face, but she was faster and pushed a foot between door and frame.

"Peter, it's—"

In that moment she heard her sister Anna's voice calling out, "Who is it at the door?"

Tears spilled from Lotte's eyes and before Peter could say a word, she screamed, "Anna. It's me, Lotte."

Moments later she was staring at her sister, who had an expression of total disbelief in her eyes.

"Lotte, honey, you made it home." Anna pushed her husband aside and wrapped her arms around her sister, both women bawling like babies right there in the doorframe, until Peter finally pulled them inside.

"Oh, Anna…" Lotte had yearned such a long time to reunite with her family, that now the words slipped from her brain. Everything slipped from her brain and she found herself on a dilapidated sofa, holding a glass of water in her hands, tears spilling down her cheeks.

"Goodness, Lotte, we heard about your evacuation and that you'd gone missing…" Anna hugged her so hard, she thought her ribs would crack. "I'm so glad you're here."

"Where's Mutter? And Ursula?"

"Ursula moved to Aunt Lydia's with the baby and Mutter is running errands."

"Thank God…" Lotte barely dared to ask her next question. "What about Richard? And our father?"

Anna shook her head. "We haven't heard from them."

"Which is a good thing," Peter said. "If they had been killed, your mother would have been informed." It was a small solace.

"I saw Jan dashing down the stairs, but he didn't recognize me."

Peter chuckled. "I didn't recognize you, either. Thought you're a vagrant coming to beg."

"What happened to your hair?" Anna asked.

"It had to go. Was safer to travel like this."

The bottomless agony in Anna's eyes told Lotte that her sister knew all too well. Things had happened to both of them, but if they wanted to survive, they had to bury the past, never to be spoken of again.

Ever.

"Look at the bright side, Lotte, it took you nineteen years of rebellion until you got what you wanted and became a boy." Anna made an effort to push the haunting memories away.

Lotte chuckled as the revelation hit her. "You're wrong, big sister. I never wanted to be a boy. I only wanted to do all the exciting things boys are allowed to do and girls aren't."

"Speaking of boys. Do you have news from that soldier you were sweet on?" Anna asked.

Her family had never met Johann, since he'd had to stay

in Warsaw when Lotte visited for a week's furlough last year.

"He was captured by the Ivan in January. But since then I've had no news." Her heart grew sad at the thought of the man she loved, and she clung to the hope that he'd soon be released and return to her side.

Thankfully, she didn't have time to dwell on her sadness for long, because the door opened, and her mother entered the apartment.

"What's..." Mutter dropped her shopping bag, and a dozen potatoes for which she'd probably been queuing for hours tumbled to the floor. Lotte jumped into her mother's opened arms. "Lotte, my baby. God... darling... you're here... my baby is here."

And for once Lotte didn't mind one bit that her mother still called her baby. She was alive and home again.

Thank you for taking the time to read SECRETS REVEALED. If you enjoyed this book and are feeling generous, please leave me a review.

The next book in the War Girls series is the long-awaited story about Ursula and her British pilot Tom. They will meet again after the war, but a relationship is not possible, due to the anti-fraternization rules of the Allies.

Read TOGETHER AT LAST to find out whether their love for each other is stronger than all the obstacles. The book also updates you on Richard and Katrina, Anna and Peter, Lotte, their mother, and Aunt Lydia.

Order Together at Last

And if you haven't read all the books in the series, start with the free prequel Downed over Germany.

AUTHOR'S NOTES

Dear Reader,

Lotte has experienced a lot since the first book WAR GIRL LOTTE, when she was an impulsive, outspoken sixteen-year-old teenager. She had to learn that every action bears consequences and that the world isn't black or white.

Some of you complained she was too immature and selfish in the first book – which she was. But I think she matured nicely and became an upstanding young woman in FATAL ENCOUNTER, where she falls in love with Johann, while they are both in Warsaw during the uprising.

SECRETS REVEALED is the conclusion of her story, although not completely. She will appear yet again in the next book of the series, TOGETHER AT LAST, which is the long-awaited story of Ursula and her British pilot Tom.

The Germans early in the war occupied Norway, but because Hitler considered Scandinavians to belong to the superior Aryan race, they never suffered the same brutal oppression as the Eastern European countries did.

I visited Stavanger many years ago, right after graduating from high school and the Lysefjord is still one of the most impressive sights I've ever seen, so I couldn't resist to sneak in a chapter about this majestic natural wonder. If you ever get the chance to visit Norway, it's well worth to climb up there.

As for the evacuation and later capture of the Wehrmachtshelferinnen, there's not much information around. During my research I found thousands of articles about male POWs, but the women were...forgotten.

They weren't soldiers, but neither were they civilians, so the Allies could basically treat them as they liked and often seemed clueless about what to do with them. As always the Soviets were the worst perpetrators and those women unfortunate enough to be in the Balkans or Eastern Europe in general didn't make it home. Thousands were sent to labor camps in Russia where most of them perished.

Even the Wehrmacht had not clear indication what to do with them, because the commanding officers were ordered to evacuate all female auxiliaries "in an emergency", but on the other hand, they were needed in their positions to ensure operational readiness of the troops. Therefore, if an officer evacuated the women too early, he'd be tried for defeatism and cowardice. If he evacuated them too late and they were captured he'd be tried for violating the order to keep the females safe. It really was a no-win situation for the commanding officers who often risked their own careers to protect the women by sending them home.

Midsummer night, or Sankt Hans as it's called in Denmark is a huge festivity, marking the longest day of the year. I spent one summer in Finland where this may well be the biggest celebration of the entire year. Under Nazi rule it was forbidden, but as soon as the war was over, the Scandinavians took to their traditions again.

Just when I had settled for a title and my fantastic designer Daniela Colleo from stunningbookcovers.com had made the perfect cover for this book, I found out that Roberta Kagan already has a book with the exact same title in her Eidel's story series. Since I didn't want any trouble, I offered to use another title for my own book, but the incredibly generous, warm-hearted and talented Roberta graciously told me not to worry about it.

So my thanks go to her, for being so kind and I wholeheartedly recommend her books to everyone who loves to read Holocaust novels. Despite the awful topic, her books always carry a sliver of hope. You can find them here: http://www.robertakagan.com/

Tami Stark, my editor, and Martin O'Hearn my proofreader made this book the best it can be by cleaning up typos, unclear sentences, or anachronistic terms. There still may be mistakes that slipped past them and if you find one, please let me know.

My biggest thanks go to you, my reader. Thank you for following the lives of my War Girls, for your wonderful emails, the encouragement, and the kind words. I love hearing from you!

If you're seeking a group of wonderful people who have an interest in WWII fiction, you are more than welcome to join our Facebook group.

https://www.facebook.com/groups/962085267205417

Again, I want to thank you from the bottom of my heart for taking the time to read my book and if you liked it (or even if you didn't) I would appreciate a sincere review.

Marion Kummerow

From the Ashes (Book 1)

On the Brink (Book 2)

In the Skies (Book 3)

Historical Romance

Second Chance at First Love

Find all my books here:

http://www.kummerow.info

CONTACT ME

I truly appreciate you taking the time to read (and enjoy) my books. And I'd be thrilled to hear from you!
If you'd like to get in touch with me you can do so via

Twitter:
http://twitter.com/MarionKummerow

Facebook:
http://www.facebook.com/AutorinKummerow

Website
http://www.kummerow.info